The two men stood ready, pointing their guns at Slade.

"That's silly," Frank said. "I'm not goin' anywhere."

The tall one smiled, heaved in relief, and said, "Well, we got you. I'm William B. Masterson. They call me Bat. I'm under sheriff in Dodge City. This is my deputy, Hank Hardin."

"Who's sheriff these days?" Slade asked.

"Charlie Basset," Masterson said.

"I've heard of you, Masterson," Frank said.

"Yeah. I've heard about you too, Slade. You got a big name in Dodge City.

"Good, we should have some nice chats on the way back," Slade said, flashing Masterson a sarcastic smile.

Bat moved closer, laid the barrel of the Henry rifle along Slade's cheek, rubbed the cold steel back and forth.

"We ain't gonna have no chats, Slade. Talk to yourself. *Talk to God,* 'cause you're gonna hang soon."

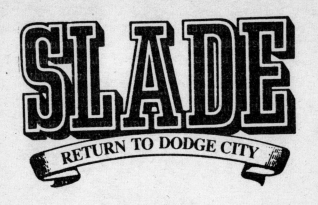

SLADE
RETURN TO DODGE CITY

Link Pennington

LYNX BOOKS
New York

RETURN TO DODGE CITY

ISBN: 1-55802-139-6

First Printing/May 1989

This book is published by Lynx Books, a division of Lynx Communications, Inc., 41 Madison Avenue, New York, New York, 10010. The name "Lynx" and the logo consisting of a stylized head of a lynx are trademarks of Lynx Communications, Inc.

Printed in the United States of America

0 9 8 7 6 5 4 3 2 1

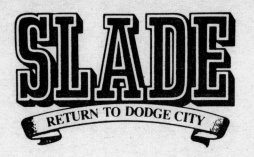

Chapter One

Frank Slade rode his Appaloosa up a steep bluff, circled a small ravine, and surged to the top.

He stood in the stirrups, rolled the kinks out of his neck and shoulders, then relaxed back in the saddle. He pulled a jar of mink oil from his saddlebag, removed his Colt .45, and massaged the thick gel into his holster.

Slade had to play all the odds.

He worked the oil in good, until the leather was soft, slick, ready.

Robbing a bank was dangerous business.

Frank checked the gun's cylinder, punched in six bullets. He didn't believe in the five-shot myth. A man who knew how to handle guns, understood them, didn't have to worry about a pistol going off in his holster.

He fed his Winchester rifle fifteen slugs, levered a

shell into the chamber, and slid the rifle back into its slipper.

Sweat poured from Frank's face. The blue bandanna around his neck was sopping wet; his clothes sticky and grimy.

Slade took a bag of Durham and some roll paper from his Levi's jacket and fixed a cigarette. He patted his pockets until he found a small box of Russel and Warrens Lucifers, then fired up.

Frank untied his kerchief, flapped it open, mopped his face. He took a long pull on the cigarette and gazed into the valley at Rochford, Dakota Territory. Slade had been in Deadwood the year before during the big strike at Montezuma Hill next to Rochford. Now, almost a year later, there were over five hundred people in the valley and many more along the adjacent hills.

Slade sucked the fire dangling at the end of his cigarette down to his fingers, then flipped it into a pile of rocks. He grabbed his canteen, knocked down another drink, and leaned back in his saddle against the cantle.

He was tired. Tired of running from the law, crooked marshals, trumped-up charges, bounty hunters, and Cliff Langdon's hired killers.

The Rochford Bank was the new building at the end of the main street. The town had a solid line of stores covering the sidewalk. Stamp mills for quartz mining jutted from the hills on the far side of the village.

Slade hadn't robbed a bank since the time he'd returned to Dodge City and taken the money he'd figured Cliff Langdon owed him for stealing his parents' land.

He thought about that night. How he'd beaten Langdon, robbed his bank, scarred him up so the crooked land dealer would never forget that he'd hired the killers of Slade's mother and father. Taking Langdon, robbing the bank, had been an act of dignity, character, justice. But it was also the reason Frank was on the run.

Slade corked his canteen and urged the Appaloosa down the bluff. He rode slowly into town. He had no plan. Plans include mistakes. Frank figured he'd go in, check it out. Then he'd make his move. Timing. That was the secret. Always had been. You could have a fast draw, but a sharp mind gave you the edge, made you a slick second faster than the other man.

Living on this edge kept Frank Slade alive.

Did he worry? Did he care?

No.

He was already wanted for murder and theft in Kansas and murder in Dakota and Montana. What could one more crime mean?

But did he care?

Yes.

Frank cared about the robbery, getting away, and he cared about his life. Cared about dignity, character, and justice.

Slade pulled up, swung out of the saddle with his saddlebags, and reined in at the hitching bar. The street was deserted. Too hot to be out. Temperature boiling. Frank ambled his lanky frame up three steps onto the board sidewalk and pushed into the bank. Two men leaned over a huge black safe that had *Halls Safe and Lock Company* scripted along the top.

Slade pulled his gun, leaned on the counter, and pointed. "Good afternoon, gentlemen. I've come to rob your bank. Make a move and you're in your grave."

Both men froze. They peered over their shoulders at the handsome cowboy who stood behind them holding the shiny Peacemaker. Slade was dressed in Levi's jeans and jacket and a black shirt. His black flattop Stetson sat low on his forehead. His face was tanned, square cut, the skin tight over prominent bone structure.

"You! The one with the bag of money," Slade said. "Bring it here to me."

The older man walked slowly to the counter.

"Would you be Buttknob?" Slade asked.

"I would."

Buttknob, the owner of the bank, had a bristle of whiskers. His face was round, jowly, and his fat tummy splashed at his vest, leaving a chunk of white shirt curling out between the bottom of the vest and the top of his trousers.

"Then you'd be the man I need to talk to," Slade said. "And you! The other man! Walk over here, make it slow, put your hands on the counter. That's right. Up here. Right in front of me. You too, Buttknob."

Slade opened the bag and dug into the gold coins. He held his six-gun on the men and carefully counted and stacked the coins.

"I'm taking ten thousand dollars, plus a thousand in interest—my commission. Eleven thousand in all. It's the money you owe the miners out along the creek. You cheated on their loans. They want their money back, and I'm here to collect."

"How dare you," Buttknob growled.

Slade glared at him. "You stole this money. I'm stealing it back."

The banker was enraged. "I'll have you sent to prison for this."

Slade grabbed Buttknob's string tie and twisted until the banker choked. "No you won't," Frank whispered.

He punched Buttknob. The banker sprawled to the floor and slid into the safe. Slade counted the rest of the money, then cracked his gun barrel into the clerk and watched him crumble.

Buttknob sat on the floor, his head resting on the wall by the safe. He went to his vest and yanked out a derringer. Slade pumped a slug into his shoulder.

"Jesus!" Buttknob howled.

"I'll be goin' now," Frank said with a smile. "Nice doin' business with you."

Slade holstered his gun outside the bank, tied the saddlebags to his rig, and trotted the Appaloosa slowly to the edge of town. He spurred a fast gallop into the Black Hills.

Frank pushed the horse through tall jack pines, around a mountain base, down a long drop into a valley, and followed a rushing stream to the Rapid Creek mining encampment.

Calamity Jane was waiting for him.

Slade dismounted and handed the saddlebag full of gold to Calamity. "I just robbed me a bank." He smiled. "This is the full ten thousand. I took a thousand commission. My price for doin' business. I gotta live, Jane."

"I knew you'd take care of things. I wouldn't have got you involved had it not been for my sister and her husband. She was a hooker with me, Slade, back when we were following General Hooker's troops, takin' care of the men. She's tryin' to make good with this fellow here in Dakota."

"Everyone can pay off their claims legal now. Buttknob will be out of it," Slade said.

"I reckon that was the idea." Jane smiled.

They stood for a moment. Slade relished the big smile

on Jane's face. "You're a good man, Frank," she said. "Now where?"

"Dunno."

"They'll get a posse out after you."

"Probably."

"Don't you be goin' through Deadwood. I told you that woman, the one who stole your money over in Montana, lost it all. Lost it gamblin' in the Number Ten Saloon. That's why she's workin' in that dance hall over in Lead. She's broke."

Frank nodded.

"You'd just ride into trouble, Slade. Take my word. They still have a warrant out for you there."

Slade mounted his horse. He looked down at Jane. "I'll be seein' you, Martha," he said.

"Oh, yeah, that's for sure, Slade. That's the truth."

Frank heeled the Appaloosa and galloped down along Rapid Creek. He figured he had a good lead on the posse. He could stop in Rapid City, pick up some nitrate caps, then make a hard ride to Yankton, on the Missouri River, and catch a steamer south. Yankton meant freedom.

Chapter Two

Everyone thought the town of Custer would be the hub of the Black Hills. The Custer Minute Men had been organized there to fight the Indians who still rode in fringe groups. They'd opened a public school in 1876, the first in the Hills, and set up a Provisional Superior Court, which was to have jurisdiction over the Black Hills.

Jurisdiction over Frank Slade.

Custer faded when gold was discovered in Deadwood Gulch. The streams around Custer were playing out anyway, and so Deadwood took on the reputation as the center of the Black Hills.

But Slade knew Rapid City would live on as the real capital of the Hills. It was the gateway to the Wild West and sat on the edge of the Black Hills, where the plains met the mountains.

Frank rode into town through a dusty sundown. Wood

buildings lined the street. Tents and wagons, miners on their way up into the Hills, surrounded the business area.

Slade quartered his horse at the livery and checked in at the Casey House. He took a bath, smoked a cigar, dressed in a fresh pair of jeans and black shirt, and walked the back alleys to Peterson's Gun Shop. He didn't have a lot of time. A posse would be after him by now, but he needed some more nitrate caps.

"Slade," Old Man Peterson said, his round, whiskered face cracking a big smile. He stuck out his hand and Frank shook it.

"I'll bet you came for more nitrate caps, huh?"

"You bet right on that, Mr. Peterson. More than one time they have saved my life."

"I thought they'd be handy, Slade. Come in. Come in," the old man said, pulling Frank into his store. He locked up and led Slade to his workshop.

"Been hearin' a lot about you, Slade. You've been doing some damage out there."

"Thanks to you, Mr. Peterson. The swivel rig you made for me was a great idea. It cuts down on my draw time like you said it would, and the nitrate caps. Well, they've—"

"I heard how you blew the hell out of a couple gunfighters over in Montana."

"I need some more," Slade said.

"I figured you would." The old man smiled. "Follow me."

He led Slade to his desk and opened a drawer that was filled with nitrate caps, little explosive devices that looked like sewing thimbles.

"I made 'em up special knowin' you'd probably be back for more, Slade."

"Same stuff?"

"Potassium nitrate, charcoal, and sulfur. You just light the fuse."

"They work great," Frank said.

Peterson waved his hand. "Take 'em."

Slade emptied the drawer into a sack Peterson held, then reached for his pocket.

"No way you're gonna pay, Slade. Me knowin' your pa and knowin' what happened down there in Kansas. The caps are yours, and here's a couple sticks of dynamite. You stay in business."

Frank remembered a line he'd learned from Wild Bill Hickok. "I've never killed a man who didn't deserve it," he said.

Peterson came out from behind the desk. "I been workin' on a new gun, Slade."

"Yeah?"

"I've cut down a Charles Goodnight Winchester," Peterson said, showing Frank the gun. "You might remember this, Slade. Came out back in 1873. Damn good gun. Fine lever-action rifle. See these factory pearl inlays? The steer head and star is signed *Ulrich*. The Goodnight was one of the best Winchesters ever made."

Slade tried to remember. "Goodnight?"

"Sure. One of the biggest names in the West. You were just a boy down in Kansas. Remember all the buffalo back then, millions of them on the plains? Back before they were slaughtered?"

"Sure do," Slade said.

"Then the Easterners came out here hunting off trains, shooting 'em just to see 'em fall. They cut the buffalo down to nothin'."

"I remember." Slade nodded.

"Goodnight was the pioneer of the Goodnight-Loving Trail, the trail that opened Texas to the cattle industry at Fort Dodge and Abilene. He was the one who took it on himself to save the last five hundred buffalo. He took 'em down to his ranch in Texas. He'll go down as a great American, Slade. And he had the rights to a fine gun.

"Anyway, I cut this barrel down, kept the lever action, the nice slope, the fine structure of the stalk. Real good for an underhanded grip, up-close shooting. I made it a combination pistol and rifle."

Slade inspected the gun, his hands sliding over the weapon carefully.

"I made a scabbard for your horse so you can carry it, or you can wear it low on the hip in this other holster I made for you."

Slade laid the Goodnight combo on the workbench.

He examined the scabbard and the side holster.

"This is fine workmanship, Mr. Peterson."

"I broke 'em in good mink oil. They're real nice, huh?"

"Yes."

"See how the holster hangs off the plate, like a swivel rig. You can shoot from it."

"I noticed."

"But I'd use this for close-in gunplay, when you're rushin' or on the move shooting. It's accurate and deadly."

Slade slipped the gun into both the scabbard and holster, slipped it out, felt the easy slide.

"I've conditioned that gun too. It's compatible with your Colt .45 slug. You don't hafta carry any extra ammo."

"It's a mean-looking weapon," Slade said.

The old man chuckled. "Meaner'n sin. You bet. Better for you to work with, Slade. I know what you're up to out there. I see what you're doin'."

"What do you mean, you know what I'm doin' out there?"

"You're angry about the way things are in the West. You want justice. You want to kill the killers."

Slade handled the Goodnight Winchester. It felt good. Real light and fast. "I like it," Frank said.

Peterson smiled. "Anything else I can do for you, Slade?"

"I just robbed a bank up in Rochford, returned some money to folks a crooked banker cheated."

"Good. Where you headed now, then?"

Slade almost told Peterson, then remembered he could trust no one, not even the old man who loved him like a son. "Don't know yet," he said.

"I understand, Slade. You tell me, they could torture me, make me spit it out."

Frank fingered several gold coins in his pocket.

"Don't pull that gold out, Slade. I ain't takin' money for this," Peterson said. "Does my soul good to know I'm a small part of Frank Slade."

Frank corrected him. "A *big* part."

Peterson walked Slade to the door and out on the porch. The moon hung low off the top of the hill.

"Need anything, just let me know," Peterson said.

Frank extended his hand, gripping the old gunsmith close to him. "I will, and thanks again, Mr. Peterson."

"Aw, get the hell out of here, Slade."

Frank angled the back alleys to Main Street. He stopped at Hanson's General Store and bought some jerky, beans, and three boxes of ammunition. Then he headed back to the Casey House.

Frank would have liked to do some drinking, maybe see a woman, relax a little, but he knew a posse would be on his trail shortly.

Maybe the Goodnight would help his odds.

Chapter Three

S lade made his own trail through the desolate Badlands, working his horse over the barren sand,
around the colored buttes and rocks.

He could have detoured around the rugged area, but
it would have taken him two days more to make Yankton, and even more important, Frank figured the Badlands would be a good place to lose a posse.

He edged the Appaloosa between boulders, galloped
over dry washes, weaved through strange-looking bones,
arrowheads, snakes, desert rats, all the time leaving an
easy trail to follow. He wanted the posse to know exactly
where he was headed.

He finally found a cluster of boulders in a ravine between two mesas. He was tired, worn down, and needed
some rest, so he stopped and made camp.

Slade unsaddled his horse, unhooked the bridle, and
patted the Appaloosa on the neck. "Sorry, old boy, no

food for you until we get to the Cheyenne.'' He tethered the horse to a rock, then sat down and ate some jerky and a can of beans. He washed it down with whiskey.

There was a long ride ahead, all the way across Dakota Territory to Yankton in the southeast corner. He could board a riverboat there and take it down the Missouri past Sioux City, St. Joe, Kansas City, then over to St. Louis, where he would book passage on the Mississippi to New Orleans.

The next morning Slade rode into the heat in a blue chambray shirt, a pair of tight Levi's, and his soft black boots. He felt good. He'd returned the miners' money, stopped Buttknob, and made a nice chunk of cash in the deal.

Frank felt the presence of the posse behind him. He never knew exactly why he always got the intuitive feeling. He couldn't have them trace him all the way to Yankton. He'd be trapped waiting for a riverboat south. He'd have to make a stand, cut them off. He heeled the Appaloosa, riding in deep sand so the posse could track him.

Slade moved slowly, letting them catch up. Just before dusk, he turned and rode through a slim needle eye into a thick canyon of rocks, mesas, and purple spires. He left heavy hoofprints leading to the opening.

Frank dismounted, walked the horse over the boulders, and found a big flattop rock. He took the saddle off his Appaloosa, hid the horse behind the rocks, and cupped him water from his canteen.

Slade crawled to the top of the rock. He sipped whiskey and checked around. He guessed the posse would reach the needle opening about sunset. They would find his tracks and ride in for him the next morning.

When the moon hung like a marshal's badge—bright, glowing, casting a shimmering glow on the Badlands—Slade pulled his new Goodnight from the scabbard and started back toward the canyon opening.

He moved quietly, a lynx in the moonlight, running, crouching, leaping over rocks, his body tingling with anxiety.

Frank smelled the campfire before he saw it. He slowed up, crept closer, slid down on his belly, and crawled along a ledge above the fire. He counted six shadows.

He lay silently, watching, listening to the men talk and laugh. They were drinking coffee, warming at the fire. Slade clutched his Goodnight Winchester. It would be a cold night, but in the morning, before sunup, when the men were asleep, he'd attack.

Slade waited until a ripple of orange shaded the sky in the east. Then he crawled the ledge and dropped down a rock shoot to the ground near the posse's camp. He crept closer, reached the perimeter of the camp, and waited.

A blanket of clouds lifted. The sun peeked through. Slade charged.

"Time to rise and shine, boys!" he yelled.

The posse jerked from their makeshift beds, stiff and surprised. One man reached for a pistol. Slade fired and knocked him back on his saddle. Another man rolled out of his blankets and came up shooting.

Frank took a hit in the ribs. Blood splashed into his blue shirt. He kept running, levering the Winchester, killing the man who had winged him. The other men were stunned. Slade stood over them, the barrel of his rifle smoking.

"I'll kill more if I have to," Slade said.

He felt weak. Dizzy. The wound in his side gushed. It felt like a slug in the ribs.

The men saw the bleeding. They tensed and sensed an advantage. Another man lifted a rifle under his blanket. Slade saw the barrel before the man could squeeze off a shot. He sent two slugs into the deputy's chest.

"Tie each other up!" Slade yelled. "Get to it or die."

The three men left got up. Frank held on, kept a watch on how the knots were tied. He checked the ropes for tightness and strength. The man who had tied up the other two turned to Frank.

"You men should be ashamed that you're riding for a corrupt town," Frank said.

The deputy yanked at his gun, taking a chance Slade's bleeding had weakened him. Frank pumped his new Goodnight Winchester and sent three shots deep into the man's belly.

"There's two of you left," Slade said. "You'll find a way to get yourself loose. When you do, go back and tell that banker in Rochford to forget about me. Tell him Frank Slade did the right thing. I gave the money I robbed to the miners. You got that?"

The men nodded.

Slade mounted one of the posse's horses, scattered the rest, sending them galloping into the Badlands, then rode bareback into the canyon. He made it to his camp through sheer determination and guts. He saddled the Appaloosa and mounted.

Slade was weak and his side ached, but he had to move fast. Keep going. But he'd lost blood and had to fight a nagging dizziness.

He held on, worked with his mind to stay conscious

and blot out the pain that throbbed in his sides and tingled up into his shoulder and down his left arm.

Slade stayed in the saddle, at times sliding off to one side, almost hanging, but he made it out of the Badlands and arrived at the Cheyenne River. He fell off the horse and crawled to the water.

But before he could drink he blanked out.

The sun burned Slade's face when he awakened. He struggled to his knees, ripped his shirt off, and inspected the wound. No slug, but the skin was gashed to the bone.

He crawled to the river. The Appaloosa grazed by the water. Frank grabbed the stirrup, pulling himself up. He took the whiskey canteen off the horse and staggered to the river.

The water bathed his wound. Slade stood for several minutes in the cool flow of the river, letting the current clean his deep cut, then he stumbled to shore, sat on a rock, and splashed the wound with whiskey. He gritted his teeth and shuddered as the alcohol hit the exposed rib.

He passed out again.

Frank came around and bent over the river, cupping his hands, tossing water on his fevered face. He threw up, heaving what little he had in his stomach into the Cheyenne.

"I gotta gut it out," Slade whispered. "Stay calm, stay calm."

Survival was an art in the West, and Slade liked to think of himself as an artist.

He lay back in the sun and removed his mind from the pain—saw himself well, whole, walking in a fancy suit through the French Quarter in New Orleans, saw himself with a beautiful Southern belle. His wound healed, just a scar where his rib sculpted into the tight ripples of his stomach.

Frank dozed. He felt peaceful, relaxed. His mind had outflanked the pain. He fell asleep thinking about Yankton, riding the river, the wide Missouri.

Slade woke up hurting. His body cracked in pain. He walked to his horse, worked the cinches loose, and knocked the saddle to the ground. He pulled down his blanket roll and made a place near a cottonwood where he could doze in the sun.

Sleep came quickly, but Slade awakened in the middle of the night. A cold Dakota wind shivered through him. He wobbled to the river and drank. The Appaloosa nosed up beside him and lapped the water. Slade petted the horse's neck.

"We're gonna make it," he whispered. "We're gonna make it, old boy."

Chapter Four

Slade walked the Appaloosa. He didn't want his wound to open and bleed. He found a place to forge the Cheyenne, then headed east. He had no idea how many days had passed or whether another posse was after him.

Frank gained strength with each mile. He was riding now, back in the saddle. Horse and man ran through the hot sun, into the cool night. He came to Ft. Hale on the Missouri River, a new fort named for Captain Owen Hale of the Seventh Cavalry. Hale had recently died in an Indian skirmish. Slade snuck wide of the fort and followed the bluffs.

Dakota was desolate country. Trees, except in the Black Hills, were a rarity. But along the Missouri, huge cottonwoods spread long branches and afforded Slade cool shade and cover as he angled the channel south.

Frank saw the Indians in a curve on the bluff up ahead.

They were specks on the top of the river. Slade had heard the Sioux had been restricted to the Rosebud and Pine Ridge reservations to the west. These Indians would have to be renegade Sioux, another handful who had refused to give up their land to the U.S. government.

Slade rode the edge of the river, angled around the bend where the Indians waited for him. He drew his Goodnight from its slipper and cocked it. He held it in one hand, loose on his knee, the stalk cocked upward.

The Indians rode in a wedge toward Slade. They were dressed in shabby buffalo skins. They had army rifles and sat tall on their ponies.

Slade recognized their leader immediately.

It was *Red Dog*!

Frank's mind turned back in time. He remembered last year when he'd killed Red Dog's scouting party on his way to the Black Hills. But he had freed Red Dog. Later that same summer, Slade had been taken prisoner by the Sioux in the northern Black Hills. Red Dog had returned the favor and let Slade go, but promised if they ever met again it would be death for one of them.

Frank reviewed the facts: Red Dog spoke English. He'd been educated by a white woman the Sioux had captured. He was courageous, and he had a vision that the Sioux would roam Dakota free.

Slade reached a clearing and stopped. Red Dog and the five braves pulled up ten yards from him.

"Red Dog," Slade said.

The Indian smiled. "My white friend. Still scavenging Indian country."

"I'm on my way out of here. On my way to Yankton."

"Another white settlement named after my people.

—20—

The Yankton Sioux. You steal our land, build towns, use our names.''

Red Dog's brown face was troubled. His teeth were bone white, his long braids black as dirt. His hair was parted in the middle, and the braids hung down over his shoulders in front. He wore a buffalo vest and buffalo skins on his legs.

"You spared my life once, Red Dog," Slade said.

"And you spared mine."

A crow swooped in over them and let out a caw.

"So, we meet again," Slade said.

"Times have changed since I saw you last. My people have been taken prisoner by the white government. They are being held on reservations. But I have not given up. Many braves ride with me."

"What about Sitting Bull?" Frank asked.

"They followed him to Canada. Chased him across the border. No buffalo there, no food. The Sioux starved. They came back. The armies were too big. There's not many Sioux left. Our leader, the brave Sitting Bull, is on display with Buffalo Bill's Wild West Circus."

Red Dog grunted, laughed, mocked.

"That can't be true," Slade said.

"But it is, my white friend. It is."

"So, now?"

"We have held out." Red Dog smiled. "We never give up."

His braves nodded. The cottonwoods leaned over them. The river rolled a swift current.

"If I die, I'll take you and at least two of your braves with me, Red Dog," Slade said.

"Stories about your gun have reached far, Slade."

"Then you'll let me ride on. I have no quarrel with you or your people."

Red Dog lifted his hand and the wedge of Indians opened. "Go," he said. "Go to Yankton."

Slade rode slowly past the ragtag braves. His intuition bubbled. He turned just in time to duck the knife Red Dog had twirled at him.

Frank leapt from the saddle with his Goodnight Winchester. He knocked three Indians from their horses. Red Dog jumped from his pony and ran for a boulder. Slade lifted to his knee and pumped off another shot into one of the braves.

He rolled quickly behind a tree. The other brave was still on his horse. He galloped at Slade, firing his rifle, splattering bark from the cottonwood.

The brave dove from the horse. Slade pulled his Eagle knife from inside his boot and plunged it into the red man's belly. The brave was skewered on the blade, his face wild with death. Slade pushed him aside and peeked around the tree. He yelled at Red Dog. "That was plain cowardly goin' for my back!"

Silence.

Slade knew Red Dog was waiting in the boulders back from the river.

"We can settle this with no more killing!" Slade shouted.

No answer.

Slade levered the Winchester and crawled toward the river, wiggled on his belly through the tall grass, snaked his way along the shore.

"Down here by the river, Red Dog. I'm down here. Come and get me!"

It was a good move. No way now that Red Dog could

come up behind Frank because of the river. The Indian would have to attack straight on.

Slade was coiled for action.

"I can't believe you'd throw a knife at my back!" he hollered.

More silence.

"There was no need for this killing, Red Dog!"

Frank waited, peeking up over the weeds. "Come on, Red Dog. I'm down here by the river."

Why didn't he make a move? Slade wondered. Then he realized that Red Dog could have moved to the river while he was crawling to the grass.

Slade rolled over.

Red Dog came out of the Missouri like a prehistoric animal, his arm cocked with a tomahawk. He tossed the ax and lunged at Frank.

Slade ducked to the right. The tomahawk grazed his shoulder as it spun past him. He fired the Winchester. Once. Twice. Three times. Red Dog took a slug in the belly, another in the chest, the third near the heart. But the brave kept coming.

Frank levered the new gun, pumped off two more shots into Red Dog. The Indian stumbled forward and fell beside Slade. Frank stood up. Red Dog lay facedown. Slade rolled him over with his boot.

"Like I said, Red Dog, there was no need for this," Slade whispered.

"Yes, there was," Red Dog managed to say before he died.

Chapter Five

Slade's wound had opened, and he was cut on his shoulder. He stuffed his bandanna into his shirt, against his wound, and headed back along the river, past the Whetstone Indian Reservation and the Whetstone Agency. It sat on a plateau a quarter mile back from the Missouri and looked heavily garrisoned.

The bleeding stopped, but Slade's side still hurt. He cantered his horse around Fort Randall, and just before sundown pulled up on a scenic bank overlooking the river.

Yankton was spread out below him on the edge of the Missouri. The *Julia Swain*, a three-deck sternwheeler, was paddling southward, spraying water. The side of the boat reflected off the calm surface of the river.

Slade rode into town, past the spacious homes built by riverboat captains, houses with gingerbread-trim cupolas, where the wives could wait for their returning heroes.

Yankton had a permanency. Dakota had become a territory in 1861, and Yankton had been named the capital. The chalkstone houses, the huge mansions, had been there since the town's beginning in 1858 when the first white settlement was constructed on an old Ihanktonwan Indian camp, after the Sioux tribe was moved to the reservation with their leader chief Smutty Bear.

Slade trotted his Martin chestnut along a dirt street near the river. He hunted for Sanford Coulson's River Transportation Company.

Frank saw the famous *Far West* steamboat docked at a landing. The *Far West* had been under government contract during the Indian wars and had served as General Terry's headquarters.

Slade pulled up and admired the beautiful steamer. After the Custer Massacre the previous summer, the *Far West* had carried Major Reno's wounded from the battle area to Mandon, 710 miles north, and done it in a record time of fifty-four hours.

Frank heeled the Appaloosa past the Episcopal church at the corner of Walnut and Second, and came upon a crowd of people pushing in around a hanging platform.

"My God, it's Jack McCall," Slade mumbled.

It had been Slade who had caught and subdued McCall the previous summer in Deadwood after McCall had back-shot Wild Bill Hickok in the Number Ten Saloon.

Slade slid out of the saddle and walked up to a well-dressed man in a black derby and gray business suit.

"What's goin' on?" he asked.

"They're carryin' out the sentence. Judge Shannon put McCall to death for the killin' of Wild Bill."

The crowd quieted. McCall climbed the stairs to the hanging platform. A black cloth came down over his head, a noose was looped around his neck, and a preacher said some words. Then the trapdoor opened.

Clunk!

The man next to Slade turned and said, "Served the bastard right."

"Could you tell me where the River Transportation Company is, sir? I'd like to buy a ticket south."

"You don't have to worry about a ticket, lad. River traffic isn't what it used to be since the railroad came in. Shame, too. I hate the noise of those damn trains." The old man took his derby off, mopped his face with a linen hanky. "You know, once we had over thirty boats a week dock here in Yankton. But it's been fallin' off. It's those big damn noisy trains."

"You mean I can just go down, buy a ticket, and board?" Frank asked.

"Sure can. There's a sternwheeler south tomorrow. Take that river road."

Slade mounted his Appaloosa, found a livery stable, and checked into the Riverfront Hotel. He had a rush of comfort about a good steak dinner and a long night's sleep.

He went to his room, threw his possibles on the bed, and washed up in a tin basin on the chiffonier. He shaved, shampooed, then carefully washed his wound, cleaned the tomahawk cut on his shoulder, and lay back on the bed.

He took a long nap, then got up and pulled his black outfit from his valise. He slipped into clean balbriggans, shirt, and pants, then pulled on his boots. He added his black coat and went to the dining room.

Pretty LaRue sat alone at a table on the far side of the room in a beautiful red dress with a décolleté neckline that lifted her tits in a dripping cleavage.

Her dark hair was parted in the middle and hung naturally on her shoulders. The bangs on her forehead enhanced the classic structure of her face.

Pretty chewed salaciously on a piece of pheasant. She held the leg inches from her mouth. Her lips were slick and juicy. She smiled at Slade and tilted her head.

Slade walked over.

"It's been a while, Pretty."

"Since your shoot-out with Pueblo in Horseshoe Flats."

"When you nursed us both back to health in different parts of the hotel."

Pretty smiled. "Sit down, Slade. Join me."

Frank pulled a chair and slipped into it, looking over at Pretty LaRue, into her beautiful face and sparkling eyes.

"Still on the run?" Pretty asked.

"You like a good joke, don't you, Pretty?"

"Where you headed?"

"South. And you? I thought you were goin' to Denver, become a big star at the Brown Palace Hotel."

"Didn't work out. I got an offer now in St. Louis. A real break."

Slade ordered the deluxe T-bone with potatoes and tomatoes. The waiter brought him a bottle of Sweet Home and he poured himself a shot. Pretty ate slowly, chewing on the pheasant, pulling strings of tender dark meat from the bone with her teeth.

"Always meant to ask you, Pretty, why you kept both of us alive—I mean me and Pueblo—after the gunfight, after we'd shot each other. You didn't tell either one of us the other was alive.''

"It was best that way, Frank."

Slade remembered those hot afternoons when Pretty would come to his room, check his gunshot wound, then straddle him and make love, work on top of him in slow undulations as he lay still beneath her, afraid his wound would reopen.

"Guess you know Pueblo and I met up again," Slade said.

"And you killed him."

Slade nodded and sipped at his shot glass.

"It's good to see you, Slade," Pretty said, her voice seductive, inviting.

Slade's steak arrived and he put it down, then sipped coffee with Pretty. She was more beautiful than he remembered her in Horseshoe Flats.

"I was always hopin' we'd meet up again, Slade."

"Me too."

Pretty leaned across the table. Her breasts bobbled in the tight lift dress. "Should we go to my room?" she whispered.

Pretty led Frank out of the dining room, up the stairs to the first floor, down the hall, and unlocked the door. She took Slade's hand and walked him to her bed. She turned and put her arms around him.

Slade slid his hands down her back and plunged his fingers into the slope of her fanny.

Pretty's tongue swirled into Slade's mouth like a slick-licking whip. Her hips rotated on his lifting hardness. He needed this. She felt good. Slade's tension was replaced by a delicious new energy.

There was a frenzy of button popping, a harmony of whispering clothes against naked skin.

Slade took Pretty down, lay her naked on the bed. He mounted her and pushed in.

"We don't need preliminaries, that's for sure," Pretty whispered.

"You were never much on 'em before," Slade said.

He sawed slowly. Pretty set her feet flat on the bed, cocked her knees apart, then gyrated up against Frank's thrust.

"God, Slade! Just do it!" she cried.

Frank answered with quick, hard jabs, his lean body pounding up and down. Pretty hooked her legs around him and pulled him in deeper.

"Damn, Slade! It's been a long time."

"I've never forgotten what you did for me back in Horseshoe Flats, Pretty."

He looked down into Pretty's face, the glow in her eyes, the way her mouth was unhinged, her tongue curled to the corner of her lips.

"So long." She sighed.

"I know," Frank whispered.

Pretty bounced wildly. She stiffened, sucked in a gob of air, then let out a long sigh. She shuddered and fell back on the bed.

Slade kept stroking.

Pretty twisted her head from side to side on the pillow, her dark hair swishing on the clean, crisp linen.

"Yeah, don't stop!" she called. "That's it, Slade! Keep it up! Ride me, damn it! Ride me!"

Slade worked her good, stayed with the flow, took Pretty to the edge, held her there for what seemed like a million years, then hammered up and down.

Pretty squirmed. She wrapped her arms around Slade's shoulders, pulled him into a gulping kiss, as her fingernails cut into his back.

"Now, Slade! Again! Now!" Pretty wailed.

But Slade had different ideas. It had been too long since he'd had a woman.

His body was like a loose rope. He worked on top of Pretty, pumping slowly again, slugging in and out with long, sure strokes.

"Oh, God, Slade!" Pretty panted. "Don't tease me."

Frank buttoned her lips with a warm, tender kiss and kept rocking.

"Put your hands under my ass," Pretty whispered, breaking their kiss, her voice trembling with passion.

Slade slid his hands under Pretty and cupped her chubby rump.

"Yes, like that, Slade," she cried.

The sound of their lovemaking filled the room. Pretty tightened her legs around Frank. She slid her hands down his back and bounced up and down. They were both lost in a hazy excitement.

"Come on, Frank! Come on!" she called.

Frank picked up speed.

"All right! Okay!" Pretty sobbed.

She pumped her hips wildly, then stiffened again. Slade felt a warm glow consume him. He bucked harder, faster.

"Gawwwd! Slade!" Pretty yelled.

Slade released all his frustration, his confusion, and madness in a blinding moment of bliss. Pretty clung to him. It was if they were suspended above the creaking bed.

Frank finally crushed down on top of Pretty, huffing,

puffing, the wound at his ribs echoing pain in counter-point to the exquisite pleasure he felt.

Pretty lay with him until Slade rolled off. She got up, lit a coal oil lamp next to the bed. Slade watched her walk to the valise. She bent over. The curve of her body excited him. She pulled out a pink dressing gown and slipped into it, then bent over the bag sexily.

Frank's cock responded, but by the time he was fully hard again, Pretty stood over him pointing a Remington .41 over-and-under derringer at his erection.

"I'll blow it off, Slade," she said.

"Aw, come on. What is this?" Slade grumbled, swinging over to the edge of the bed, sitting up.

"One more move and I'll blow your privates to hell," Pretty warned.

"What's up, Pretty?"

"You aren't anymore, that's for sure." Pretty smiled, and held the gun steady.

"You put in with Langdon. He sent you after me, didn't he?"

Pretty backed slowly to the door and unlocked it. Two men barged in. One had a Navy Colt in his belt and carried a fancy Henry repeater with deluxe Hargrove Factory engraving on the hardwood stock. The other man pointed a sawed-off shotgun.

"You're under arrest, Frank Slade!" the tallest man shouted. "We're takin' you back to Dodge City to stand trial for murder and bank robbery!"

Slade looked at Pretty. She was dressing, ignoring him.

Both men wore stars. They manacled Slade's wrists and ankles. He pleaded with them to let him dress.

"You'll stay naked until we leave for St. Joe," said

the tall man. "Then we're goin' back across Kansas so you can stand trial in Dodge."

Slade sat submissively. Pretty finished dressing. She walked to the door and turned. "Be careful. He's tricky," she said, and walked out.

The two men stood ready, pointing their guns at Slade.

"That's silly," Frank said. "I'm not goin' anywhere."

The tall one smiled, heaved in relief, and said, "Well, we got you. I'm William B. Masterson. They call me Bat. I'm under sheriff in Dodge City. This is my deputy, Hank Hardin."

"Who's sheriff these days?" Slade asked.

"Charlie Basset," Masterson said.

The lawman was handsome. He had a prominent mustache and black hair.

"I've heard of you, Masterson," Frank said.

"Yeah. I've heard about you too, Slade. You got a big name in Dodge City, bein' a hometown boy and all."

"Good, we should have some nice chats on the way back," Slade said, flashing Masterson a sarcastic smile.

Bat moved closer, laid the barrel of the Henry rifle along Slade's cheek, rubbed the cold steel back and forth.

"We ain't gonna have no chats, Slade. Talk to yourself. *Talk to God*, 'cause you're gonna hang soon."

Chapter Six

Slade sat naked in locked chains. The lawmen stood over him, guns pointed, until Masterson finally relaxed and leaned against the wall.

Frank figured the odds. He had to work with his mind so he wouldn't reveal the horrible panic he felt. He'd wait for a split second in the loop of time pulling around his neck, find a slip in the knot, and escape.

The horrible sight of Jack McCall dangling from the end of a rope, his neck snapped, his head twisted to the left, his body limp, flashed through Slade's mind.

Later on, deep in the night, when no one was about, Masterson and Hardin walked Slade, still in chains, to the river. They took him up a gangplank and into a steamer, pushed him down in the belly of the boat, and secured him in a small compartment.

"You takin' me down the river?" Slade asked.

"To St. Joe," Masterson said. "Then we'll ride back across Kansas to Dodge."

"Isn't there a train now?"

"Sure, but we're ridin', Slade. Takin' a train would be too risky. You might have friends who could try somethin'."

Slade lay down in a small bunk. The irons on his ankles and wrists rubbed against his skin, but he needed rest, needed to clear his mind, focus in on what was happening to him.

He closed his eyes and thought about Pretty LaRue. *The little whore. How could she do that to me? Money, of course, and Langdon must have paid her plenty.*

Frank dozed for a while, but every time he awakened one of the lawmen sat across the room with a cocked gun.

"How 'bout some clothes?" Slade asked Masterson.

"You looked cute naked," the under sheriff quipped.

Slade leapt from the bunk, but tumbled to the floor in his tight irons.

"Get up!" Masterson shouted. "And don't go gettin' no more ideas like that. I'll give you some clothes when we dock."

Frank crawled back on the bunk, closed his eyes, and tried to calm himself. He used the hypnotism technique he'd learned from The Pueblo Kid, thinking of a blank picture, something like a fresh, white sheet, while he waited for an idea on how to escape.

The boat docked in St. Joe.

Masterson and Hardin took Slade's chains off, let him dress in a pair of Levi's and jacket, gray shirt, and his own boots. Frank could tell by the fit of his right boot that they had lifted his Eagle knife. They had also confiscated all his possibles, his money, guns, and saddlebags.

The lawmen marched Slade along the hall, then down a flight of steps to the deck of the riverboat. A throng of gawking people crowded the landing.

"That's him."

"There he is."

"That's the one."

"Frank Slade!"

"It's him."

"Not as old as I thought he'd be."

"Jane, there's the man that killed all those men."

"I thought he was younger."

Slade had become a minor legend at twenty-eight. Masterson and Hardin pushed him along as if he were a lost steer, roughed him up, acted big. Slade hated them. He hated the people staring at him, whispering about him. They didn't know how it had all happened, back when he'd committed the crime that had sent him on the run.

Slade hobbled in front of Masterson and Hardin. The two lawmen were living in glory.

Frank was dying.

He lifted his head, chin jutting, and looked straight ahead, his green eyes flashing. He dragged his chains through a narrow path wedged between the gossiping crowd. Masterson pushed him up the steps of a jail and took him to a cell.

Masterson disappeared, but a man stood guard outside his cell, and another was posted at the door to the front office.

Masterson and Hardin returned the next morning, fed

Slade beans and bread, led him outside, loosened his leg irons, but kept his wrists manacled. They pushed him up onto a sorrel and handed Slade the reins. The deputy mounted and rode in front of Slade. Masterson stayed about five lengths behind.

Frank rode west, out into open flatland. There was time to escape. He could lay plans. There had to be a way.

Chapter Seven

Slade looked back over his shoulder. "You gonna keep me chained all the way?" he yelled.

Masterson cradled his Henry in his arm, the barrel pointed at Frank. He rode behind Slade, off to the side of him.

"You'll do as we say, and you'll keep your mouth shut," Bat shouted back.

"A man like you, Masterson, a reputation like you been building, all the stories about you in the papers, it's gonna go slack on you when people hear the truth about me."

"Plug it!" Masterson snapped.

"People will hear my side finally."

"Listen to him, Bat," Hardin interrupted, "and after what he done to Langdon, how he robbed the bank, killed a guard."

"That's Langdon's story!" Slade shouted.

"Hold it! Stop!" Masterson commanded.

Slade pulled up. Hardin held his shotgun on him. Masterson rode slowly to Slade, nosed his horse around in front, and faced Frank.

"I'm doin' my job here, Slade. You got your problems, I got mine. They ain't the same. If you're innocent, you'll get a chance to prove it."

"That's a laugh." Slade smiled.

"Okay, Hardin," Masterson said. "You'll have to follow up on Mr. Langdon's advice, I guess. I'll turn my back this time."

Hardin chuckled and knocked Slade from his sorrel. Frank hit the ground and rolled over on his back. Hardin kicked him in the balls.

Hardin's jaws were covered with black whiskers, his nose bulbous, his eyes ice blue.

Slade spit at him.

Hardin sneered and gave Frank another boot. This time Slade screamed in pain.

"Now we're gettin' somewhere," Hardin said, chuckling. Then he kicked Slade again. His toe caught Frank in the ribs and opened up his bullet wound. Hardin watched as the blood oozed against Slade's gray shirt.

Masterson came over. "That's enough. He's got the point. Let him back on his horse."

Hardin laughed and picked Slade up, lifted him like a toy, then heaved Frank up onto his saddle. Frank slumped forward, both hands groping for the horn.

"We got directions, Slade, to bring you in without regard to your condition," Masterson said.

Frank nodded, gasped, and tried to catch his breath. He wanted to vomit, wanted to pass out, but he squeezed the saddle horn and hung on. Hardin slapped Slade's horse into a walk, picked up the reins, and tossed them to Frank. Slade clutched the straps, pulled out the slack, and moved forward.

Masterson and Hardin were intense and thought they had a worthy goal: take Frank Slade to Dodge City, bring him back to his hometown, and hang him.

They rode west from the Missouri, through bluestem grasslands, cantered the slope of the Great Plains, and followed the shallow, meandering Smoky Hill River. They angled the bank downstream from Junction City, winding through bottomland groves of cottonwoods, ash, elms, oaks, and hackberry.

Days were hot and humid. Nights were windy and cool, but soft in texture. The prairie moon bathed their campsites in a shimmering halo.

Slade's ribs shot pain down his side, up into his chest and arm. He'd stopped bleeding, but now he'd have to go through another healing.

He thought about Pretty LaRue. If he made good an escape from his current dilemma, he would, from this day on, be more observant in every saloon he visited. He'd be on the watch for her. He'd thought they had unfinished business after the shootout in Dakota, but now there was a score to settle with Pretty.

The lawmen herded Slade along the river. They cut up to the tracks of the Kansas Pacific Railway as they moved toward Abilene, a booming cattle terminal founded over twenty years before by the enterpriser and promoter of the Kansas cattle trade, Joe McCoy. The "Real McCoy."

Abilene had sat on the border of the Civil War, half Yankee, half Confederate. Slade was too young to care.

Masterson and Hardin took him through the huge herds of cattle surrounding the town: tired longhorns just up from Texas, thousands of wild animals bound for northern and eastern markets, four-legged beef that brought big money to Abilene and Joe McCoy.

McCoy had built his reputation as the originator of the frontier cattle market slowly but carefully. Now he was the king. Slade remembered reading McCoy's book a few years before. McCoy had boasted about the idea of opening a trail to market for Texas cattle and providing a place where the Texans could terminate their herd, bargain with eastern buyers, and then celebrate the profit.

Cattle. Grazing land. Money.

The very reasons Slade had left Kansas on the run.

Slade's ribs ached. His body sobbed with pain. He rode in front of Masterson and Hardin into Abilene, past the stockyards, the barns, the office building, the livestock scales, past an elegant hotel with a livery stable attached.

Slade gave thanks that the sheriff's office and jail sat out by the stockyards. He wouldn't have to be paraded through the streets of Abilene—a small favor from Fortune's Wheel.

Frank spent the night behind bars. The irons were back on his legs, and his hands were locked together. He tossed to the right and the left, and twisted on the hard rock floor.

There had to be a way. He had to escape. He just hadn't thought enough about it. Slade kept his mind clear, trying to stay alert for the chance that might free him.

His wrists were raw. His ankles hurt. He tried to remove his mind from the pain and sleep, but he would have sworn he'd been awake all night by the time Masterson appeared before sunup and put him back on his horse.

They rode south out of Abilene, down the Smoky Hill, to Humbarger's Ford cattle crossing, then on west. The sun burned at Slade. The going was slow because of his condition and the irons that held him. There were moments when Frank felt a wild panic, as if he were a wounded deer trying to outlast the pursuing hunters.

Masterson smiled when they made Ellsworth. "Gettin' closer all the time, Slade," he said.

Ellsworth was another town that had grown up around a military encampment. It lay before the riders just a mile west of the fort on flat land between round bluffs that were met by a riverbank and big cottonwoods.

"We'll bypass town, take him on down to Fort Larned," Masterson said.

"How come, Bat?" Hardin questioned.

The three riders sat on a bluff overlooking the busy cattle terminal.

"Too dangerous," Masterson mumbled.

"How's that, Bat?" Hardin asked.

Masterson turned to Slade. "He's got friends here," he said, sliding a toothpick into his mouth.

"Friends?" Slade said, a laugh echoing from his mouth for the first time in days.

"Yeah, friends," Masterson said. "Know a guy named Arlen Olson, Slade?"

Slade did, but said nothing.

"Used to be a boyhood friend of yours. Right, Slade?" Masterson said, sliding the toothpick from one corner of his mouth to the other, brushing it over his hairy upper lip.

"Yeah, you bet you know him. He lives in Ellsworth. Might be if we took you into town Olson could make a move."

"That's such bullshit I can't believe you said it," Slade mumbled.

But Frank thought back. If there was one person who might help him it would be "Doc" Olson, his old friend. The Olsons had had a farm near the Slades in the early days.

Masterson took the toothpick from his mouth, flicked it off into the wind. "You gotta remember, Slade. Nothin' you say matters."

He turned to Hardin. "Let's move it out."

Fort Larned was one of several military forts established to protect the Santa Fe Trail. It was positioned on Lookout Hill overlooking the Pawnee River and was home of the 19th U.S. Infantry.

Frank rode ahead of Masterson and Hardin into the fort. He looked around for a possible escape. There were four big twelve-pound Mountain Howitzers positioned at the corners of the parade grounds.

The officer quarters were situated on each side of the commander's house and the barracks were rowed up across the quadrangle. The buildings were all one story and made of sturdy sandstone. A young officer greeted Masterson, and Slade was taken by three troopers to a guardhouse.

He walked into the cell, hobbled in his chains to the bunk, and sat down across from a young boy.

"Where they takin' you?" the kid asked.

"Dodge."

"What for?"

"They're gonna hang me," Slade said.

"They're probably gonna shoot me," the kid blurted out loudly.

Slade looked up at him. Just a boy. "Why? Why would they shoot you?" he asked.

"I ran. I chickened out. We had a skirmish with the Kiowa, and I took off."

Slade lay back on his hard bunk.

The boy broke into tears. "I been here weeks waitin' for my court-martial. This has been hell. A real hell."

Frank thought over his own situation. "So, we're both goin' through our own hell," Frank said.

"I'm a coward," the boy bawled.

"How old are you?" Slade asked.

"Seventeen."

"Shit," Frank mumbled.

"It's not so much I'm a coward, really. I just couldn't kill nobody, even an Injun. I just couldn't squeeze the trigger."

"So, what the hell are you doin' in the infantry?" Frank asked, sitting back up in his bunk bed.

"My old man. He made me join."

"Why?"

"He said he wanted a son in the army, help build the country."

"Oh, Jesus!" Slade sighed.

"They gonna hang you, really?" the kid asked.

"If I don't find a way to escape."

"They got you all chained up."

"Like an animal in a trap," Slade added.

The kid lay back on his cot, sniffling, blubbering.

"Get yourself together, for Christ's sake," Slade said. "Whatever you do, don't let 'em see you're scared."

Slade lay down again and tried to get some sleep, but

the young soldier whimpered all night long, and before sunup Masterson was leaning over Slade again, pulling him off his bunk.

"One more day, Slade. We're almost there."

Slade looked at the kid. He was asleep, his mouth unhinged, his face grotesque, and he was snoring loudly.

Slade faced Masterson. "This is gonna be a mark on you, Bat," he said. "The truth is gonna get out when you take me back."

"You keep it buttoned. No more talk. None. I don't want another word from you, Slade," Bat said, unlocking Frank's leg irons.

Late in the afternoon, Slade, Masterson, and Hardin pushed their horses up a steep incline to the top of a bald bluff.

"There she is. The Queen City. Dodge," Bat said, a warm smile cutting across his face.

Hardin nodded, pulled on the brim of his brown Stetson, then spat a spray of tobacco.

The Arkansas River snaked below them, along the base of the bluff. Buffalo grass waved in the prairie wind and stretched for miles, out to where the land and the sky merged into a pink haze.

Dodge had grown since Slade had sneaked back into Kansas and settled his score with Cliff Langdon. There had been astounding changes since he'd moved with his parents to Kansas in 1867.

Masterson lit a cheroot, smoked it slowly, and sat hunched over his saddle horn. Slade stared down at Dodge. He saw a lone buffalo humping through the bluestems. The beautiful sight made Slade remember that this part of Kansas had started as a mecca for buffalo hunters.

This was back when he was a kid, when more than two hundred thousand buffalo hides had been shipped in the winter of 1872.

Slade saw Masterson and Hardin following the wild strut of the buffalo. Masterson said, "Too bad we don't have a Sharps so we could pick that sunabitch off."

"Wasteful killin' is what ruined the buffalo," Slade said. "Back when I was a boy there were always carcasses strewn on the plains out here."

"I thought I told you to shut up!" Masterson snapped.

"I'm so sorry," Frank said sarcastically as he remembered what his father had told him: *"One day, son, the buffalo will be gone. Then what will happen out here?"*

Cattle, of course.

Dodge was a natural, and in 1874 the Santa Fe Railroad built a stockyard. Shipments were small until 1876, when Cliff Langdon had Slade's mom and dad killed, then stole their land.

Langdon had gambled on Dodge City becoming a major terminal for Texas cattle. He needed land.

Early in 1877, the Chisolm Trail to Wichita came under quarantine legislation, and the Santa Fe built an even larger stockyard at Dodge. Businessmen, mostly Easterners who had come West to make their fortune, reduced prices of liquor, tobacco, and hotel rooms, making Dodge an attractive stop on the Santa Fe, a terminal that would become more important than Wichita.

Slade rode with his captors on the edge of the lush grassland, which was crowded with cattle fattening before loading at the Santa Fe pens.

Dodge was surrounded on all sides by huge herds of Texas beef waiting for shipment to Kansas City, Omaha, and Chicago.

They curved into town at the prostitute cribs. Slade saw Donna Hand, the most famous soiled dove in the West. She had been working the cribs when Slade was a teenager and had given him his first taste of sex.

Donna saw the procession. She stepped down from her porch and yelled, "Slade! That you, Slade? Remember me?"

Frank nodded, smiled, and Donna waved.

"They finally got you, huh, Slade?"

"For now," Slade shot back.

"Can it!" Masterson yelled.

They rode down Front Street, past a group of women in walking dresses. A cold silence split the afternoon. People stared as Slade passed the Longbranch, F.C. Zimmerman's Hardware, T.L. McCarty's Drugstore, the Saratoga Saloon, G.M. Hoover's Dry Goods, and several new saloons that had not been there last summer.

Frank glanced to the right, then the left, saw folks from the old days, back when Dodge was a tacky settlement near the army fort.

He noticed hundreds of new faces, more Easterners who had moved West to supply the demand for cattle products. These people were merely curious. They didn't know Frank, but the hometown folks gawked at the man they remembered as a gangly kid.

Slade recognized Bill Turner and his wife Emily, Chalk Beeson, owner of the Longbranch, and Hannah Butler, another soiled dove who had been working the cribs for over ten years in southwestern Kansas.

Frank kicked his leg out of the saddle and slid to the ground in front of the sheriff's office. Masterson locked his ankles in the iron cuffs again and pushed Frank through the crowd. The sheriff of Dodge City, Charlie

Basset, stood on the steps of the jail. He smiled and greeted Bat Masterson.

"Good work, Bat," he said.

Ed Masterson, Bat's older brother and marshal at Dodge City, smiled proudly. "Damn right, Bat. Real good work."

They took Slade to an isolated cell in the back of the jail. The place was empty, as Frank expected it would be. They had moved the other prisoners elsewhere.

Slade would be a *special* guest.

He felt a hand press into his back, then push and punch him into the cell.

An iron door slammed shut with a hollow *clink*.

Chapter Eight

Many times in the past Slade had envisioned his fate. Now the worst had come true. He shuddered, almost like a dog shaking off water, took a deep breath, and hobbled in his leg chains to the back of the cell.

He looked around his cell. A cot, a pail of water, an empty pail for a toilet, and one thin towel. Then he peered through the barred window.

A guard stood outside his cell in the alley. People were still gathered up on Front Street.

Slade's capture was big news.

The noose was tightening. Time running out. Death coming down. Frank hobbled about his cell. It was strong and sturdy. He couldn't find a way out. Besides, what could he do with his legs and hands in irons?

He went to the front of the cell, clutched the bars, and looked down the hall that led to the front office.

There was another guard sitting on a stool beside the door.

More panic.

Slade didn't mind being on the run. There was a certain freedom to it—alone in the West, always on the move, meeting new people, winning new battles. But being in a cell made him shiver with fright for a moment. He shook it off, calmed himself down, and tensed his flow into one thought.

Escape.

Frank paced until sundown, then he yelled at the guard. "How 'bout an oil lamp, something to read? Got a *Harper's*?"

The guard ambled down the hall. He was a cretinous human being. He pushed his belly up to Frank's cell. "Huh?"

"A light. Something to read."

"All you get is this light in the hall. It's enough to see. I ain't got no instructions for readin' material," the guard said, and walked back to his position at the door to the sheriff's office.

It was late the next morning, after Slade had awakened and lay on his cot for hours, when Abby Dalton arrived.

She stood in the hall on the other side of the bars. "This is far enough," the guard said.

Slade got up from his cot, pulled his shirt around him, and buttoned it.

"I'm your attorney, Mr. Slade. Abby Dalton."

Frank tucked his shirt into his jeans and took a look at the pretty young woman. She had thick brown hair spiraled on her head in frilly lifts, with strings of hair hanging around her neck. Her lush body was sheathed in a very proper but tight blue dress. Her face radiated a troubled beauty.

"My lawyer?" Slade asked.

"Under Kansas law someone has to represent you. I'm the only one who would take the case."

"I see," Frank said, his eyes hot on the way Abby's dress bulged at her chest with the lift of her fine breasts.

"I should also confess, Mr. Slade, this is my first case."

Slade walked to the small window and leaned against the rock wall of the cell. "First case?"

"I came here from Kansas City last spring. Dodge is growing. There's lots of legal business here."

"But no one wants to give it to a woman, so you took my case."

"It's more difficult than I thought it would be here in Dodge, but I'm able to support myself. I'm the school-teacher here too."

"What's the use of all this anyway? They'll hang me. The jury will be rigged."

"You can't be sure about that, Mr. Slade."

"If you don't know that much, you shouldn't even be here."

"I know Mr. Langdon has great influence here in southwestern Kansas, but I hardly think he would tamper with the jury."

Slade chuckled. "You have a lot to learn about Dodge City."

"Be that as it may, I intend to represent you at the trial."

Abby pulled a chair from the wall and sat down in front of Frank's cell. "My first question is easy. Did you do it? Did you rob the bank and kill the guard?"

"Yes," Slade admitted.

Abby Dalton opened a leather notebook and started scribbling. "You want to plead guilty?"

"I want to tell my story. How it happened. Why I robbed Langdon, how the guard was killed. Cliff Langdon had my parents killed. He took our farm. Stole our land."

Abby wrote furiously as Slade related the entire story. When he had finished, Abby said, "I'll have to think about all this. You had a good reason to do what you did, but proving Mr. Langdon ordered the killing of your mom and dad, then took your land, will be tough. Even if we prove that, you still robbed the bank and killed a guard. It will be difficult to get an innocent verdict. You may have to do time in prison no matter what we accomplish at the trial."

Slade chuckled. "Prison time? Hell, they'll hang me. No way I'm gonna get a fair hearing in this town."

"Trust me, Mr. Slade. Give me some time. Let me think how I can best approach this problem."

"When will they have the trial?" Slade asked.

"Soon. They've called a judge from Wichita."

"He'll be on Langdon's payroll too," Slade said.

"Oh, I hardly think so, Slade."

"Listen, Miz Dalton. I don't want you representing me unless you realize what I'm up against here in Dodge City. Don't underestimate Langdon. He controls this part of Kansas."

"Is there anyone who can testify in your behalf, anyone who knows the story?" Abby asked.

"No, it happened at our farm. No one saw it except me. Saw how Jim Tripp and his gang rode up and killed my ma and pa."

"And then you killed Tripp and his men?"

"From the barn. It was easy, except for two men who came into the barn first, but I got them too. I dragged them into our house, buried my mom and dad, set fire to the house, and escaped south to Texas."

"And you were only seventeen?" Abby asked.

Slade nodded.

"This is going to be difficult," she said.

"Impossible."

"Give me a chance, Slade. Trust me."

What could Frank do? Abby Dalton was all he had, but he knew why she had been assigned to his case. She was a woman. She would be easy to defeat. The trial would be a sham, but the papers, the record would read that Frank Slade had had a proper representation and a fair trial.

What bullshit, Slade thought. He peered through the bars outside his window to the guard, the people up on Front Street, the wagons, the horses.

He turned back to Abby Dalton, his last link to life, and asked, "Do you believe my story?"

"I have to. I'm your lawyer. We've got problems here. Mr. Langdon has made a sensation out of your capture, and so has Bat Masterson. Masterson wants to run for sheriff. It's assured he'll be elected now that he's brought you in. Langdon wants to be governor. We have to keep that in mind."

Frank walked across the cell, back to Abby. He slid his fingers around the bars. "The odds?"

"The truth?" Abby whispered.

"The truth."

"If I were a card player and knew something about poker, I'd never be in this game."

"That's what I wanted to hear," Slade said, giving Abby a big wide smile. "Let's do it. Let's take 'em on. Maybe we can hit a straight."

Abby left and returned the next morning. She became a frequent visitor to the hallway outside Slade's barren cell, taking notes on everything he told her, working out the defense she planned to present in court.

Frank viewed the entire process as a blur. Unless he could escape there would be only one way out of Dodge City, Kansas.

In a coffin.

Chapter Nine

A howling wind whipped the side of the jail. Slade sat on his cot in the same stinky clothes he'd been given back in St. Joe.

He was caged, and it made his blood boil. He got up, took his shirt off, washed it in the pail of water he'd been given, gave himself a bath, washed his pants, hung the clothes across a bar in the cell, and sat down in a pair of gray balbriggans.

The hallway door opened. Slade looked up and saw Cliff Langdon waddling toward his cell.

A simmering loathing shook Frank. He stood up and faced Langdon. The banker assumed a conceited stance, cracked a supercilious smile, and said, "It does me good, Slade, to see you locked up like this."

Slade clunked across the cell. "You're *ugly*. I did that to your face," he whispered.

"You're gonna pay for it too."

"I should have killed you, Langdon."

"Your mistake, Slade."

"You murdered my mom and dad. You took our land."

"See how you lie," Langdon said.

"You sent Tripp to see us."

"Who's Tripp?"

"One of your men."

Langdon smiled. "Never heard of him. He around? Can he testify?"

"I killed him."

Slade clutched the iron bars, moving in his chains, pressing against the cell door at Langdon. "You ordered the killings, Langdon."

"Why do you keep tellin' people that, Slade? I never did such a thing, never would have. You keep tellin' that story. Now, we'll get the truth out."

"You needed our land. Purely greed. You needed a point near the Pawnee to take in Texas cattle. I'll give you that. You sure saw the future."

Langdon's scarred face wrinkled into another smile. "That's 'cause I'm smart, Slade!" he said.

Slade trembled. He wanted to reach through the bars and strangle the crooked banker.

"I'll find a way out of this, Langdon, and when I do I'll kill you."

"Not unless you know magic, Slade. But you'll never find a way out of this. You're hooked. You'll never send me another marshal's badge. Never again will you soil my reputation. You've been a frustration. Now you're dead meat, just like all those cattle I got grazin' on your parents' land out there by the Pawnee."

The pudgy banker flashed Slade a toothy smile. His belly pressed against his fancy suit.

Slade flushed with hate.

"You're going to hang, Slade. The rope is twisting around your neck."

"And you'll be governor," Slade growled.

"That's right. You'll be up there in Boot Hill, and I'll be runnin' the state."

Frank lunged at the bars. His arms shot through at Langdon. The ugly banker backed up, turned abruptly, and wiggled back down the hall.

"Guard! Guard!" he yelled. "Slade is getting violent!"

Frank paced the cell, tried to work the venom out of his soul, but fell frustrated and shaking on his cot.

Abby Dalton came every day the first week. She filled three notebooks with information about the case. A second week passed, and the night before Frank's trial she visited him.

She sat in a chair by the bars, dressed in a black skirt and pink blouse. Her legs were crossed, her black boots laced tightly.

"I want you to know, Frank, that I believe you. I believe your story, and I intend to win this case."

"How?"

"We'll put you on the stand. You said you wanted to tell your story."

"They'll say I'm lying."

"That's why it's important we go over everything, all the details. We go to court in the morning."

Slade was surprised. "Tomorrow?"

"I didn't want you worrying about it. The trial will be a circus. Papers from Kansas City, Wichita, and Topeka have sent reporters. People have come in from all over the state. They're scalping tickets for seats.''

''Tomorrow, that's when they start the hangin' process, then,'' Slade mumbled.

''You don't have enough confidence in me, Slade.''

''It's just that I understand this town, and I don't think you do.''

Abby got up quickly. She walked to the bars. ''We'll plead guilty with *justification*. That's our defense. You came back to Dodge to claim what legally belonged to you . . . your land. You had to kill the guard. It was self-defense.''

''What about the beating I gave Langdon?''

''There we'll rely on the mercy of the court and hope they understand your frustration. Why you did it. You'll tell your story.''

Frank walked to the bars. Abby pressed her face forward. Slade's lips met hers between the cold iron bars.

Frank pulled away. ''Let's not get anything started that's gonna end with my hanging.''

Abby stepped back. ''I guess you're right. That was unprofessional of me.''

Silence for a moment, then Abby said, ''With our defense there's a chance there won't be a hanging, Slade. Just prison time.''

Frank went back to his cot. ''I'll tell my story. The rest is up to you, Miz Abby.''

Chapter Ten

Masterson and Basset led Slade from the jail and walked him along Front Street.

Slade held his head high, maintaining his dignity as well as he could, exuding a confident arrogance, as he plodded along in choppy steps, dragging his irons.

People pushed down off the board sidewalk for a closer look. Masterson and Basset walked behind Slade, rifles pointed at him, parading him past the Santa Fe Depot to the courtroom.

The crowd had already judged and convicted him. Slade could see it on their faces.

"Mrs. Dickel," Frank said, nodding to Ethyl Dickel, a woman he'd known when he was a lad. He remembered how Ethyl had come to their farm and swapped hot dishes with his mother.

"Barney, Cal, Miss Price," Slade said, calling their names as he dragged his irons in passage.

Frank wanted all of them to remember this day, how they waited and watched for his hanging like it was a sideshow.

Slade hobbled to a table at the front of the courtroom. He slumped into a chair beside Abby. Marvin Bailey, the prosecutor, and his assistant, Lyle Young, sat at the table to Frank's right. Bailey was a short, wiry man with thick glasses and a handlebar mustache.

Abby wore a black dress with a high white collar. She radiated confidence.

A noisy rush filled the court. The crowd scurried in and jostled for their seats.

The bailiff introduced Judge Bill Lynch, a tall but bent man with a silver circle of hair ringing his bald dome.

Bailey opened the trial with an emotional presentation to the jury. "You are all upstanding citizens of Dodge City. This trial goes back to our roots, back to the days when we lived on farms and small ranches around the fort.

"There sits Frank Slade. Most of you know him, or you know of him. Some of you remember him as a boy. Let your conscience decide Slade's fate. Forget that he's from Dodge City. He was never a part of our progress and growth. Mr. Slade left as a youngster, then returned a little over a year ago, came back in the dark of the night, stayed in town for almost a week as he planned and calculated his crime of murder and robbery. His crime of assault and attempted murder against Cliff Langdon. Yes, I said *planned* and *calculated* his crime before he slipped down an alley to Cliff Langdon's, robbed the bank there, killed the guard, and severely assaulted Mr. Langdon.

"That's the Frank Slade on trial here today. That's the Frank Slade who sits here at this trial. Frank Slade the bank robber, Frank Slade the murderer, a sadistic killer who scarred Mr. Langdon for life.

"The state will present witnesses who will testify about what happened that night in Dodge a year ago. You'll hear from Mr. Langdon himself. You'll hear from Ed Beeler, one of the guards on duty the night Slade robbed the bank. The state will prove Frank Slade is guilty, and you will have only one decision to bring to this court after your deliberations.

"Guilty as charged."

Bailey sat down and Abby Dalton rose from her chair.

"Mr. Bailey is quite eloquent. I'm sorry I don't have a long narrative instruction for you as he did."

Abby walked to the jury box, placed her hands on the railing, leaned in, and continued. "Frank Slade's defense is simple. He did what he did because he had to do it. He did what he did to regain something that had been taken from him and his family. Their farm! He did it to avenge the murder of his mother and father—"

"*Objection!*" Bailey yelled.

"Let's hear it," the judge said.

"It's never been established, your honor, that Frank Slade's parents were murdered, and also, let's remember who's on trial here. I request the remarks be stricken from the records."

Judge Lynch leaned forward. "Counsel is right, Miss Dalton. Keep your comments relevant."

Abby let go of the railing, walked back and forth in front of the jury, and continued. "We'll prove the murder Frank Slade is accused of was a killing in self-defense. The jury will hear the truth. We'll prove Frank Slade had good reasons for what he did. We'll prove that anyone would have considered the action Slade took if they had suffered the same loss as he did.''

Abby sat down and the trial began.

A long list of witnesses testified that Slade was indeed Slade, and this parade was followed by a rambling statement from Ed Beeler, one of the guards on duty the night Slade robbed Langdon. Beeler identified Slade as the man who killed his companion.

Langdon testified last.

''I was in my office, working late in the back of the store, which was also being used as a bank at that time, and when I left, walked out into the alley, Frank Slade jumped me, pushed me back into the office, beat me with his gun and fists until I opened the safe. He stole a sack of money, then set about beating me again.''

Bailey leaned an arm on the witness stand, his face inches from Langdon's. ''And those scars, Mr. Langdon?''

Langdon pointed at Slade. ''He did it! That man there! Frank Slade!''

Bailey turned to the jury. ''I submit that Mr. Langdon's face, the scars you see, is proof of what happened that night when Slade visited him.''

Bailey whirled quickly back to Langdon. ''That deep scar on your cheek, Mr. Langdon? Slade did that?''

''Yes, he hit me with the butt of his revolver.''

''And all those other scars,'' Bailey said, now prowling the space between the witness stand and the jury box, his hand fingering a gold chain looping across the front of his vest. ''Frank Slade did that too?''

"Yes."

"No further questions, your honor," Bailey said.

Abby walked to the stand. "Isn't it true, Mr. Langdon, that as early as 1866, when Kansas became a state, you were buying land in and around Fort Dodge?"

"That's true."

"And didn't you have a man who worked for you at that time named Jim Tripp?"

"A lot of men have worked for me over the past ten or eleven years."

"But you didn't answer my question, Mr. Langdon. Did you or didn't you have a man working for you named Jim Tripp? A specialist at what he did."

"I don't recall."

"I've checked, Mr. Langdon. I can call witnesses who will testify that you indeed had a man named Jim Tripp on your payroll."

"So what?"

"And didn't you want the Slade land out by the Pawnee River south of Dodge, that strip of land just off the Arkansas River?"

"Objection! Objection!" Bailey screeched. "There's no record of the Slades' owning land down that way."

"That's because the title to their land was stolen the day the Slades were killed. That title was stolen and changed," Abby shot back quickly.

The judge pounded his gavel. "Can you prove such an accusation, Miss Dalton?"

"I will try, sir."

"You must show legal ownership."

"I'll withdraw my comments, then," Abby said.

Bailey smiled and sat down. Abby continued. "Did

you send Jim Tripp to the Slade farm, Mr. Langdon, with an offer for their land?"

"I don't recall doing that."

"But you did. You sent Tripp and several men to make an offer for the land, and when Josh Slade, Frank Slade's father, refused to sell, Tripp and his men killed him, then killed his wife and—"

"*Objection!* She's making an assumption here, your honor. There's no evidence such a meeting took place."

"Please confine your remarks to facts that can be proved, Miss Dalton."

Abby turned from the judge, strolled back to the jury box, looked silently at the jury, turned and walked back to Cliff Langdon. She faced him straight on.

"Do you own that land now, Mr. Langdon, the plot of land on the first bend in the Pawnee?"

"No, the railroad owns it."

"Who sold that land to the Santa Fe?"

"You'd have to check the records."

"I did, Mr. Langdon. *You* sold that plot to the Santa Fe."

"*Objection!* Please, your honor, she's badgering the witness. What does it prove if Mr. Langdon sold that land to the railroad?"

The judge gave Abby a stern look. "This is my last warning, Miss Dalton. Stick with the facts. Don't try to weave a story here."

Abby continued. "On the night Frank Slade visited you, Mr. Langdon, did he not make you sign a bill of sale for that land?"

"No."

"*Objection!* There is no bill of sale."

"It was taken from Frank Slade when he was arrested. It's disappeared, your honor," Abby reported.

"Your honor, how long must we put up with this line of questioning?"

"I have no further questions, sir," Abby said.

The prosecution rested its case.

Abby stood up again. "I call Frank Slade to the stand."

Slade got up, his lanky frame lean, hard. He hobbled in his chains to the stand and slipped in.

"Your honor, I want Frank Slade to tell his side of this . . . and without objection from the prosecution. Mr. Slade has that right. Go ahead, Frank."

"I was seventeen. We'd just finished havin' dinner. My pa saw a group of men ridin' in over a knoll. He told me to go hide in the barn. He waited in front of the house. Jim Tripp and his men rode up. They said they had an offer from Cliff Langdon for our land. Pa said he wasn't interested. Tripp said it was a fair offer, that my pa should take it, and if he didn't they had ways of makin' him sign the bill of sale.

"Pa wouldn't do it, so Tripp sent one of his men into the cabin. They pulled my ma out, beat her, tore her dress. Pa told them to stop. He said he'd sign. Tripp handed him the bill of sale. My pa signed it. They asked where I was. Pa said I was visiting relatives in Nebraska. They sent two men to the barn to check. I waited. I heard shots. I knew they'd killed my mom and dad. I shot the two men when they came into the barn after me, then I leveled the rifle out the hayloft door and shot Tripp and the rest of his men. When I got down to the house, Tripp was still alive. I took the bill of sale and shot him again, killed him. I buried my folks, dragged

Tripp and his men into the house, set it on fire, then I rode south down to Texas. I worked the cattle trails for almost ten years. I practiced fast draw. I kept waitin' for the right time to come back. Then I did. I came back into town. I stayed a few days, checked out the bank at Langdon's. I went there one night to collect for our land. A guard tried to kill me. I stabbed him with an Eagle knife. I knocked the other guard out." Frank pointed to Ed Beeler. "Then I made Mr. Langdon open his safe. I took seventeen thousand dollars from Langdon's own account. That's the amount I thought our land would be worth at current prices, now that it's part of the railroad. Then I beat Mr. Langdon up, scarred his face so he'd never forget what he did to my folks. I left Dodge and rode north into Dakota."

"And you've been on the run ever since, right?" Abby asked.

"Yes."

"So, you do confess to robbing the bank, and you took only seventeen thousand dollars when you could have stolen much more?"

"Yes," said Slade.

"And you killed the guard while protecting yourself?"

"Yes."

"And you swear, so help you God, that the land in question here belonged to your mother and father?"

"I do."

"That's all."

Bailey smiled. He rose slowly, ambled confidently to the witness stand, leaned in close to Slade. "That was a mighty colorful story, Mr. Slade. You almost had me believing it. But now, let's talk facts. Is it true you're wanted in Dakota for murder, Mr. Slade?''

Slade nodded.

"What? I didn't hear you?''

"Yes,'' Frank said.

"You killed a federal marshal, didn't you?''

"But that was The Pueblo Kid. He was sent by—''

"Just answer my question.''

"Mr. Slade, just answer,'' the judge admonished.

"Yes,'' Slade said.

"And isn't it true you killed a sheriff in Montana? You're wanted there too, aren't you?''

"Yes.''

"And this, Mr. Slade,'' Bailey said, slipping a piece of paper from his inside pocket. "This is a warrant for your arrest for bank robbery in Rochford, Dakota Territory. This just happened recently.''

Slade knew the deck was stacked.

He got up and hobbled in his chains away from the stand.

"Your honor!'' Bailey shouted. "The witness is in contempt.''

"Return to the witness stand, Mr. Slade, or the court holds you in contempt!'' the judge shouted.

"You can hang me twice,'' Slade snapped, sitting down.

The courtroom buzzed.

The judge banged this gavel.

"No further questions, your honor,'' Bailey said.

Chapter Eleven

Lady Fortune's wheel was on another fast fade. Slade and Abby sat in a small alcove off the courtroom waiting for the jury to decide.

"You saw how it was rigged against me," Frank said. "I'm surprised I got to say as much as I did. But they cut you off all the time, Miz Abby."

"I did my best, Frank."

"I know, and I'm obliged."

"We confessed to self-defense. We tried to make it clear about Langdon."

"Doesn't matter. All those folks on the jury are from Dodge. Langdon will have 'em all bought off."

"Maybe not, Frank."

Slade smiled. "That's what I like about you, Miss Dalton, you're an eternal, ah . . . let's see . . ."

"Optimist?"

"Yeah, I read an article about it in *Harper's*."

"You'll be reading about yourself in *Harper's* soon, Slade. They had a reporter here."

Abby stared at Frank. Even in jail clothes he looked good: gray shirt, gray pants, black boots, his rugged but handsome face, black hair.

"Masterson is running for sheriff," Abby whispered.

Frank chuckled.

"Bat brought you in. That will get him elected."

"He wasn't a bad sort, really."

"He does have a good reputation, Slade."

"He was just doin' his job, like he told me. Thing is, he wasn't livin' around here when all this took place. He doesn't know the truth."

"He'll be elected."

"I suspect he will," Frank said.

They sat in silence for several moments, then Abby said, "What will you do when you get out of prison, Slade?"

"If I'm lucky enough to get prison out of this, if I ever go free, I'd take some time to think about that, maybe find a piece of land down in Texas, out in Montana, up in the Black Hills, stock some cattle, start a ranch. I don't know exactly."

Again silence.

"And you, Miss Dalton? Will you stay here in Dodge?"

"I'll get legal work. This trial will help, and I always have my teaching job."

Abby pulled a pint of Sweet Home from her purse. "I bought this earlier. Thought you might like a drink before the jury comes in."

Frank shook his head and smiled. "A woman who knows how to please a man," he said, pulling the cork and tipping the bottle. He knocked down three good slugs and handed the Sweet Home back to Abby. "That gives a man a jolt," Slade said.

A soft knock rapped the door. "The jury's in," came a voice.

Abby led Frank past the guard in the hall back to the courtroom.

The crowd rushed for seats. The judge took the bench. The jury filed in.

"Have you reached a decision?" the judge asked the foreman.

Wayne Hanson, a tall cattleman, got up. "Yes, we have, your honor."

"Read it."

"We find Frank Slade guilty of murder in the first degree, robbery, and first-degree battery."

He handed the decision to the bailiff, who presented it to the judge. The judge read the decision. "We could put off the sentencing if I had any question in my mind about it, but I don't. I will pronounce sentencing now."

Abby touched Frank's elbow. She rose from her chair. Frank stood up.

The judge looked down at Slade.

"Frank Slade, you are guilty as charged, and I sentence you to be hanged until dead on the morning of September 27, 1877, in Dodge City, Kansas."

There was a flurry of activity. The crowd rushed out of the courtroom to spread the news. Reporters beelined to the telegraph office. It was certain now.

Frank Slade would die.

Chapter Twelve

The next few days passed like stagnant water trickling over a broken dam.

Slade paced his cell.

Outside a funereal pounding hammered nails in the hanging platform up on Front Street. Each crack of the hammer ticked off another second Frank had to live.

He went to the small window and watched the carpenters work. He thought things over, but as hard as he tried, he couldn't come up with an idea that would free him.

A vision of Pretty LaRue holding a derringer on him kept Slade's mind occupied and confused. *Why did she do it? Why did she trap him for hanging?*

At last the hammering stopped, which was a relief to Slade, but the loop that dangled over the new platform in back of his cell sent shivers through Frank. He had to accept his fate. He would choke in front of people who had seen him grow up.

Swirls of anxiety raced through Slade's stomach. Death! Hanging! Twirling from a noose. The thought of his execution sapped Frank's will. He lay back and tried to relax, but couldn't. Then he paced the cell, worked his mind for a way out.

The door down the hall opened and closed. A Catholic priest made his way to Frank's cell. Slade got up as they let the preacher in.

"Do you want to confess, son?"

"No."

"But, lad, they're going to hang you."

Slade sat back on his cot. The priest stood over him. Frank looked up. The priest's face was rubbery and blotched with alcoholism.

"Son, you're going to die. It's time to make peace."

"I've never been a religious man, Father, and I don't aim to start at such a late date."

"But listen, lad. You'll be hanged in the morning, soon as the sun comes up."

"I guess I've come to accept that," Frank said.

"That's why I'm here, Mr. Slade."

Frank got up, walked to the window, and looked outside. The noose hung like a necklace in the shimmer of full moonlight. The guard in the alley cast a long, black shadow.

"At least let me say some words over you, son."

"I'll say my own words," Frank said. "You can leave."

"I'm a man of God. Let God help you."

"If God had wanted to help me, he could have done

it a long time ago,'' Slade said. He waved his arm toward the cell door.

"Guard!"

The deputy walked to the cell.

"The preacher wants to leave," Frank said.

A short time after the priest's visit the guard at the
door guided Abby Dalton down the hall to Slade's cell.
Frank saw her coming in the glow of the kerosene lamps.

"Just yell when you're ready to leave, Miss Dalton,"
the guard said.

Abby waited until the guard left. She moved close to
Slade's bars. Frank got up.

"It's bad news, Slade."

"You got that right, Miz Dalton."

"I've been trying for a stay of execution. I took it all
the way to the governor. They've turned us down." Abby
folded her arms and looked at Slade sadly. "I'm sorry,
Frank. I've done everything I can."

"They been hammerin' up a hangin' platform outside
my cell. Do you know who's doin' the hangin'?"

"They've called in the hangman from Hays City,"
Abby said.

A death silence screamed between them.

"I can't stay long, Frank. I want to keep trying. I'll
send off another telegram. There's still several hours
left."

"Will you be back before the . . ."

"I'll be back before morning one way or the other,"
Abby said.

Slade joked with her. "Back with good news or back
to say good-bye, right?"

Abby turned and started up the hall.

Slade sat on his cot. A calm came over him. A final acceptance. He lay back and had a nap before he was awakened by the guard.

"Got your last meal here, Slade. It's a T-bone steak with potatoes and bread."

He slid it through a slit. Slade took the tin plate and sat down with the food. He picked at it.

Last meal! Last minutes! Life fizzling out like a fuse on one of his nitrate caps. Slade wasn't able to eat. He placed the plate on the floor under his bunk and lay back.

In the middle of the night Abby came down the hall again. The deputy led her to Slade's cell. He turned and walked back to his stool at the end of the hall.

"Well?" Frank said.

"Nothing, Slade. No answer."

"Guess this is good-bye, then," Frank said.

"Not necessarily," Abby whispered.

She lifted her brown skirt over a pair of pink bloomers. She looked over her shoulder at the guard. He was reading a *Police Gazette*.

"In my underpants, Slade, dip into my pants."

"Huh?" Slade said. "This is a strange time to—"

"Just put your hand down in my underpants, Slade. Hurry!"

Frank slid his hand into the pink bloomers, dunked deep, and brought out a Red Hot Number Two .32-caliber five-shot revolver. The Red Hot felt good. Slade squeezed his fingers around the handle. The gun gave him a shiver of new life.

Abby dropped her skirt. "Is there a chance with that?" she whispered.

"Is it loaded?"

"God, Slade. Of course it's loaded."

"Why, Abby?"

"I don't want you to hang."

"You'll be ruined, Abby. You'll never practice law again."

"I don't want to if what I've seen here is the law."

"You'll go with me?"

"Donna Hand has horses for us. She's waiting behind her crib."

"You know what you're getting into, right?" Slade asked.

"As long as I'm with you, I don't care," Abby said.

Frank had lain awake many nights in his cell pondering his hanging, his situation, but on every occasion he had wondered what life would be like if he were a free man, if he could court Abby Dalton, and now she was tying herself to his fate. He leaned toward the bars.

Abby smiled. "How do we do this? How do we break you out of here?"

"The chains. The irons. We're not goin' anywhere unless we get the key to the leg irons," Slade said.

"I have it. I've been keeping my eyes open. They've kept it in a desk out front. I took it before I knocked on the door for the guard."

Abby knelt down, reached through the bars, and unlocked Slade's leg irons. Then she worked the key into his wrist chains.

"God, that feels good," Slade whispered. He shook his legs and wiggled his fingers. "I can't believe you got that key, Abby," Slade said.

"They won't either when they find out."

"Call the guard," Slade said. "When he comes back to the cell, hike your dress again, yell for him to help you. When he runs up, turn quickly, grab the barrel of his rifle, try to pull it through the bars so I can get my hands on it.''

"I hope he has the keys to this cell, Slade."

"Well, if he doesn't, you're going to be in here with me before long."

Abby called the guard. He came down the hall, his rifle ready. Then he saw Abby with her skirt up. Slade had one arm out of his cell, hooked around Abby's waist.

"*Hurry!* He's trying to rape me!'' Abby shouted. "The animal! Help!"

The deputy ran to Abby. She whirled around and grabbed his rifle. Slade was ready. He got hold of the barrel, twisted the rifle before the guard could fire, and pulled it from him.

Slade handed Abby the Red Hot. She pointed it at the guard. Slade cocked the rifle and did the same. The deputy stood defenseless. He trembled and his eyes were full of terror.

"One little move and you're dead. Either I get out or you die with us," Slade said. "The keys to the cell. Where are they?"

"I dunno "

The guard looked as though he was about to run.

"Don't move. I'll shoot you," Slade warned.

"I'm not movin'. I'm right here, Slade."

"The keys."

"Don't know."

"Sure you do. I'll give you five seconds to remember, then Miss Dalton and I are going to kill you."

"Down by the door where they've always been."

Abby took off and returned with a ring of keys. "Which one?" she asked.

The deputy fingered the keys and lifted one. "This key here."

Abby grabbed the ring.

"This is gonna go hard on you, Miss Dalton," the guard said. "Breakin' Slade out like this. You'll hang someday just like him."

"Keep your fat mouth shut. We didn't ask for comments, you ass!" Slade ranted.

Abby slid the key into the lock and opened Slade's cell. Frank grabbed the guard and jerked him inside. Abby held the Red Hot ready. Slade put the rifle down, locked the deputy in his irons, then gagged him with Abby's kerchief.

He pushed the guard to his bunk, then hammered a hard right to his chin. The deputy slumped into a curl on the cot.

"We'll leave the cell door open until we take the guard outside in the alley," Slade said.

They ran down the hall. Abby headed for the front door.

"Wait. My possibles. They have to be around somewhere," Slade said.

"On the wall, in the cabinet," Abby said, turning at the door to the street.

Slade gathered his gun belt, his Goodnight Winchester, and his saddlebags. He checked the secret slip pocket at the bottom of one saddlebag, found his nitrate caps, his dynamite, and heaved a sweet sigh of relief.

Frank hooked his gun on, settled it on his hip, cocked the Goodnight, and gave the extra rifle to Abby.

Abby hurried out onto the sidewalk. She looked up and down Front Street, then beckoned to Slade.

Frank kept his back to the front of the office, worked

his way to the alley opening. The guard was walking in the other direction.

"Go down the alley, throw him off, start a conversation," Frank whispered.

Abby straightened her skirt and walked down the alley. The guard turned. They started chatting in low voices.

Slade slid around the corner. The deputy had his back turned. Frank snuck up and cracked him in the head with the butt of his Goodnight Winchester. The deputy slumped to the dirt.

Frank dragged him back through the alley, into the jail, down the hall, and opened the cell. He gagged the deputy and left him with the other guard. Then he snuck back to the alley. "They'll both be out for a couple hours, then they'll have a hell of a time callin' for help. Should give us a good head start on a posse," he told Abby.

"Quick, down the alley, Slade," Abby whispered. "Follow me."

She led him past the backdoors of Front Street business establishments. They run through another alley, then out into the open, hiding behind houses, until they reached Donna Hand's crib. She was waiting for them, holding the reins on two roans.

"I been around this town a long time," Donna said, "and I never felt better about anything."

Slade took the reins.

"Don't say nothin' mushy, Frank Slade," Donna said. "I know what you done. I know you was in the right. Besides, wasn't I your first ever?"

Abby swung up on her horse.

Slade leaned closer to Donna. "You were my first. My very first, Donna."

"So, there's somethin' to that, right?"

Slade mounted his horse. "Damn right, Donna. There's somethin' to that."

"Go, both of you. Ride hard. Ride fast. Git!"

Donna stood behind her crib and waved as Slade and Abby galloped into the bright moonlight.

Chapter Thirteen

Slade and Abby rode across the flatland toward the Cimarron Cutoff on the Santa Fe Trail. Frank was elated he'd escaped the hanging rope, but Abby wondered what kind of life she might have had playing along with Langdon in Dodge City. Maybe she should have worked the power, staked out a career.

But another part of her, a more important part, tingled with exhilaration. Slade was innocent. She was sure about that, and even if the law saw it a different way, she knew in her heart she had done the right thing.

Abby looked ahead into the moonlight at the thin man who rode off to her side. What would he do now, how would he feel, once he'd found freedom? Would she still be part of his life?

Slade thought only about making good on the escape. The rest would fall into place. He never wasted time

—85—

worrying. It was Slade's opinion that worrying was a waste of energy.

They reached the Cimarron River and Slade waved at Abby to stop. "Can't keep pushin' the horses this hard. We're not far from the Oklahoma Panhandle as I see it. We need to rest the animals and decide our next move."

"Mexico?" Abby said.

"Sounds good, but we have to figure the safest way to go. I'd say we got a posse about four, maybe five hours behind us. We might be lucky and the guards won't be found until morning, my hangin' time."

They dismounted and Slade uncinched and unbridled the horses. He led them to the river so they could lap up the fresh, cool water. He let them slurp their fill, then tethered them to a low branch.

Abby waited for Slade under a rock bluff. She opened her saddlebags. "I brought you some clothes, some Levi's, a jacket, and a fresh shirt. I've got some jerky and biscuits here too."

Slade was grateful to get out of his prison grays. Abby watched as he stripped to his shorts.

Slade looked down at her pretty face reflecting in the moonlight. She was flushed from the long night of riding

She got up and unbuttoned her skirt and stood in front of Slade in her brown riding boots, pink bloomers, and a black blouse.

Her hair was windblown. She worked her bloomers down. Slade took her in his arms and kissed her. They knelt down on the blanket. Slade was under her. Abby straddled him, lifted up, then took him in.

"Slade!"

"That's good," Frank said.

"Real good," she moaned, rocking up and down, humping her hips slowly on Slade's rigid cock. She leaned over him, her hands on his shoulders, her hair hanging in thick strands from the sides of her head.

"We're gonna make it out of this, aren't we, Slade?" she whispered.

"We'll find a way."

"I love you, Slade. I guess I loved you the minute I saw you sitting in that cell."

Abby bucked up and down, her face inches from his, her breath hot on his mouth.

"We can find a place, make a life," Slade promised.

Abby had sacrificed for him, given up a career and a life she had studied years to live. Now she was a criminal . . . on the run with Frank Slade.

"Do you love me, Frank?" Abby whispered.

"If you'll marry me when we get to Mexico."

Abby kissed him, screwed harder, more frantically on Slade's demanding hardness. She worked her hips in slow circles. Her knees spiked into the blanket on both sides of Slade. She bounced up and down.

Frank pumped off the ground. His fingers threaded into her thick, brown hair.

"God, Slade!" Abby shouted.

Frank pushed up, humped into Abby's slow grind.

"I knew it would be good like this," Abby blurted out. "I knew it would."

They were locked together, their bodies working in soft harmony under a showy prairie moon that glowed so bright Slade could see Abby's face, her expression, the wrinkles of pleasure etched on her forehead.

A blinding, brilliant minute stood still. Slade and

Abby forgot about their dangerous run for freedom, forgot they would be hunted like animals.

Abby stiffened. She pushed down on Slade's shoulders. Her fingernails dug in. Frank arched off the blanket. He bucked fast, heaving Abby up and down with each hard pump. She held on, stayed with him, sliding on him.

"Yeah, okay!" Abby shouted. "Okay!"

They lay in each other's arms until Abby rolled off beside him and relaxed. The cottonwoods whispered above them. The rush of the river sounded like soft Mexican violins.

Abby cuddled close, whispered in Slade's ear, "That was beautiful, Frank."

Slade stared up into the heavens, the clusters of stars, the bright moon. "Yeah, beautiful," he repeated.

Abby snuggled into him. They kissed. Slade's cock responded immediately. Her soft curves felt good, especially after what he had been through.

Abby gripped his wild throbbing. She lay back, opened her legs. "Again?" she whispered. "Again?"

Slade mounted her and pushed in. Abby's legs horseshoed around him. He rocked slowly. She tickled his back and stroked him gently.

"Yes, again," she whispered. "Again, but hurry, Slade. This time, hurry!"

Abby slid one hand through Slade's hair, pulled his head down, and kissed him. Frank worked faster.

"Over. Roll over. I want to be on top again," Abby said, breaking their kiss.

They rolled on the blanket, still connected, until Abby

straddled Frank, up above him on her hands and knees. Slade ran his hands over her back.

"I like it up here," Abby whispered, her voice sultry and trembling.

Frank lifted and punched deeper.

"Ah, gawwd! Slade!"

Frank felt free. He felt good. A new energy sizzled through him. He pumped up and down off the blanket, spiking hard into Abby.

She stiffened above him and shuddered into a climax. Her mouth hung open. She shouted, "God, I love you, Slade!"

Then a shot split the night.

Abby slumped forward and fell on top of Slade. Blood spilled down her back onto Frank's hands where he held her.

Slade had no alternative. He pushed Abby off and rolled quickly to the right. He grabbed the clothes Abby had brought for him, and his Winchester, and belly-crawled to a tree.

"*Slade!* I come to get you. I know I hit you. I bet you're bleedin'!"

"You killed the woman, Hardin!" Slade screamed. "You killed Abby, you sonofabitch!"

Hardin yelled back at him. "Serves her right for breakin' you out. Lucky I came by the jail just after you left. I took off before the posse organized. Now you're trapped, Slade! The posse'll be along any minute."

Frank slipped into his new clothes. He worked his lean body into the fresh Levi's, slipped on the blue shirt, buttoned it, pulled on his boots, and slid along the trees toward Hardin's voice.

He stopped, flat on his belly, and looked over his

shoulder. Abby lay in the moonlight, limp, dead, her long hair splashed out on the ground in a halo above her head.

"I'm gonna come and get you, Hardin! I'm gonna kill you."

"Ain't no way!" Hardin yelped.

His voice came from a hill, across a wash up ahead of the trees. Slade got up, ran to the river, then raced as fast as he could along the bank. He cut back into the trees near the wash. He sprinted over the top, down into the gully, slammed to his belly, pumped off two shots at the hill, then rolled to his right.

Frank saw the report from Hardin's rifle. The lawman was on top of the hill on the other side of the wash. Slade fired again, then ran across the wash, closer to the hill.

"I'm comin' after you, Hardin!" he shouted.

Two shots pinged rocks behind Slade. He jumped a small bush and ran up the bluff where Hardin was hiding. He came up on the far side of the deputy, saw his shadow, but couldn't get a target on the man himself.

"Over here, Hardin!"

Another shot. Slade saw the orange blast. He crept closer, his Goodnight levered, ready. He advanced within ten yards of Hardin.

"Try again, asshole!" Slade yelled, leaping to the left as Hardin fired.

Frank ran toward the rocks rimming the top of the bluff.

Hardin triggered off another shot into the night.

Slade stopped when he saw the fire, held the Goodnight with one hand, levered the cock-handle with the other, and slammed off eight slugs at Hardin.

Frank reached the rocks and crawled slowly to the edge of the bluff. He found Hardin lying dead beside a boulder.

Slade walked over to the lawman, his Goodnight pistol-rifle smoking. Then he pumped the gun dry, sent the rest of his slugs into Hardin's loose body.

Frank had to hurry. There was no time for hate. Hardin was dead. That was enough. He ran back down the bluff, into the ravine, across the wash to the river. He angled back where he and Abby had made camp.

He gathered his possibles, the jerky and biscuits, went through Abby's purse, found fifty dollars in gold, then bent over Abby.

The moonlight outlined her as if she were in a natural coffin.

Frank pulled her skirt down, fixed her hair, and kissed her lightly on the lips.

Abby deserved a proper burial. Slade understood that, but what could he do? The posse would be on him any minute. He had no time for words over her if he was to save himself.

Slade saddled up and left Abby at the bank of the river, left Hardin dead across the wash at the top of the bluff. He rode into the river, stopped the roan, and let the animal drink. Frank dismounted and waded back to shore. He brushed the campsite with a spirea bush, erased his boot prints to the river, and sloshed back out to his horse.

The river was cool, clear. The moon shimmered on the rolling ripples. Frank filled his canteen, then lifted up to his horse and rode in the water, along the shallow edge of the Cimarron. He was headed west.

A change of plans.

Slade reasoned that if he could stay ahead of the posse, reach the Colorado Plateau, the high country of the Jornado, he might have a chance to make a stand.

He rode the river an hour before Abby's tragic death settled in, and then it was like a bear trap sinking its claws into his heart.

There were so many things he didn't know about Abby. He'd planned to discuss them. She knew him intimately. She had pried the details as she scribbled notes for the trial, but he had picked up only scraps of information about her.

Abby Dalton had been from the East. Educated, bright, young, beautiful. And she had given her life for Frank Slade.

Slade was a strong man, but he felt as though he were coming apart in weak, little pieces.

Chapter Fourteen

Slade followed the Cimarron River around its bend, rode south a few miles, then left the river and galloped straight west toward Colorado and into the sand hills of the Jornado.

Frank pushed the roan full speed until the horse wore down again, then he walked the tired animal. He had to ration water to both himself and the horse. The next fifty miles would be dry. No streams. No rivers. Nothing until he reached the Purgatoire River near Trinidad.

Slade stayed alert for a posse but could pick up nothing. Maybe riding in the river, along the edge in the water, had thrown them off. But Frank didn't delude himself. They could have split up, sent men in several directions.

Some of them could be on their way after him, maybe only a mile or two behind.

Slade rode and walked through the dark, then climbed

higher in the early-morning sun. He was up over six thousand feet on the Jornado.

Frank had thought the Badlands desolate. This was plain scary. Rolling, arid land. Cactus, tumbleweeds, a few cedar bushes, and long flattop mesas that looked like big riverboats.

Riverboats!

Slade would be on a riverboat bound for St. Louis if it had not been for Pretty LaRue. He plodded forward, wondering why she did it, why she trapped him and turned him in. It had to be the money. But why? Did she need money that badly? Was money that important to her?

Frank cursed the day he'd met her.

The sun broke through low-hanging clouds that dipped over mesas in the distance. They moved close to the ground, like a curtain draping the plateau.

The sun hid behind the bellying clouds. The weather turned cold. Slade could see his breath. He stopped, let his horse rest, and checked his possibles. He pulled out the Levi's jacket Abby had given him and walked the horse higher, up into colder temperatures.

Slade figured if he could make the Raton Pass he could lose the posse in the rare air of the Rocky Mountains around Trinidad. He wanted to find Simpson's Rest in the majestic Spanish peaks of the Sangre de Cristo Range, the place he'd read about, the place where George Simpson, scout and frontiersman, had hidden in the natural caves from hostile Indians.

The story was legend.

The Indians couldn't find Simpson. He moved from cave to cave, hiding and holding them off.

Slade rode all night before he reached the Purgatoire

River, the River of Lost Souls in Purgatory. Frank jumped from his horse and led the lathered animal to the water. The horse beat Slade to the river, then they both drank from the cool flow.

If the posse's mounts gave out before his roan, Slade figured he had a good chance to make his strategy work. There was no place between the Colorado line and Trinidad to buy or borrow fresh horses.

The higher Slade climbed the colder it became. Windy during the day. Freezing at night. He ran out of jerky, the biscuits were frozen solid, and the roan was limping.

What he had to do now was walk himself and his horse into Trinidad, get a room, a fresh mount, then ride up into the Raton Pass and get lost in the huge mountains for a few days before winding down into New Mexico.

Slade heard the hoofbeats of the posse coming from behind him on the Jornado. The sun was up. He looked back across the plateau and saw six riders. He'd been right. The posse split up or there would be more men. The six who rode toward him must have followed the Cimarron and picked up his trail.

The deputies dismounted and walked their horses. They were tired like Frank, their mounts worn down. Frank figured that as an edge.

He decided to make a stand.

Then the posse spotted Slade.

Frank pulled his Winchester from the slipper on the roan, pumped a cartridge into the chamber, dipped into his saddlebags, and pulled out two nitrate caps. He led the horse a few yards down the river and tied it to a tree.

The posse was too far off for rifle fire, unless some-one had a Sharps. Slade watched the six men talking things over. He knew what they were talking about. It would be murder riding straight into him. They had no protection on the plateau.

Frank ducked into the trees, worked his way along the bank of the river, and found an inlet surrounded by cottonwoods.

The posse spread out and circled him. One deputy crossed the Purgatoire to take up a position behind him. It was obvious what they had planned. They would wait for dark, then close in.

Slade had to find a way to take six men before they killed him. He figured on one advantage. The men in the posse were average citizens of Dodge City trying to do their civic duty, hoping their name would be printed in history for bringing Frank Slade back to Kansas. They had volunteered to go after Slade. They had been full of confidence when they accepted their assignment. Not one of them on his own would be a match for Slade, but six of them creeping in on him in a loop checked the odds.

Would they have the guts to come in after Slade if he made a stand? Frank figured they would. He was news. Each man out there wanted to go back to Dodge with a story to prove he was the one who had killed Frank Slade.

The night would come down black and cold. Frank gathered buffalo chips and driftwood near the river. He built a hot, wild fire with leaping flames. He wanted to let the posse know where he was, make it easy for them.

Slade got up, walked the edge of the river, and looked for a cleft in the bluff. He found one and inspected it. He made sure the indention hung out over him so the posse couldn't crawl the bluff above him and shoot down on him. He'd made that mistake before and never would again.

The posse circled Slade and worked a noose around him. Frank had a quick thought about the hanging platform waiting for him back in Dodge City.

They stopped when they had Slade surrounded, then stood out on the plateau like prison sentries.

The wind howled. Low, gray clouds kissed the Jornado. Slade figured he was up over ten thousand feet. The sun squeezed between two mesas as it dropped into the horizon.

It wouldn't be long now.

Slade had figured it. The posse would come in after dark. They had to be working odds too. But they would have to kill him if they were to take him back to Dodge.

Darkness spread over the Jornado. Slade went to work gathering more buffalo chips along the river. He threw them into the fire pit, loaded the hole with chips, and fired it back up with a Russel and Warrens stick match.

He sat down in front of the warm flames. The buffalo shit burned high and sent a pungent smell into Slade's nose.

Now was the time to lure the posse in, if they were stupid enough to think he hadn't seen them, and he guessed average men from Dodge might think that way.

Frank piled more chips on the fire, feeding the dancing flames, teasing the posse.

The men crept closer out on the plateau. They had set their timing by the hang of the moon. Slade could feel them. He had to build a rock fort in front of the cleft. He carried rocks from the river's edge to his cut in the bluff. His lean muscles pulled. His arms hung low as he lifted stones from the river, along the bank, and hauled them back to the bluff.

Slade ran farther down the river to find more rocks. Did he have time? His arms ached. His back hurt. He worked fast in the dark and constructed a wall of stone about five feet in front of the opening.

Perfect.

They had not seen him scurrying about. They thought he was sitting at a campfire unaware. At least Frank hoped they had suckered the bait.

Slade crouched behind the bunker with his rifle and nitrate caps. The little fort he'd built gave him a feeling of security. He ran back to the fire pit and tossed more buffalo chips into the flames.

The river rushed a cold whisper into the icy night. The wind calmed down. Slade was freezing behind his rock fort.

The fire spit and crackled.

The posse would have to be colder than he was, Slade conjectured. He warmed his hands in his Levi's, his rifle leveled over the top of the rocks, and his Colt .45 ready right beside him.

Slade could sense them close. "Come on, you bastards!" he yelled. "I'm right here waiting for you. I'm not gonna run. Come on in!"

Slade saw a lean shadow in the glare of the fire. A man rushed in and crouched. Frank swiveled his Winchester and squeezed off two shots.

He heard a groan and saw the man drop.

Then they came. A rush of men. They'd taken the bait. Did they think Frank hadn't seen them on the plateau circling him? Did they think he'd be sitting at a campfire on the Purgatoire waiting for his death?

"You dumb bastards!" Frank yelled.

He lit a nitrate cap and heaved it into the wagging shadows.

The explosion cracked the cold night like a hammer splitting ice.

Screams! Yells! Moans!

Slugs pinged off Slade's rock bunker.

Some were still alive. One? Two? Three? How could he know?

Frank leapt from the bunker, his Goodnight blazing, pumping bullets at dead bodies, shooting at one man who brought up the rear and was now hightailing it along the river. Slade stopped, beaded on him in the moonlight, pulled the trigger, and hit him. The deputy chucked forward and tumbled like a jackrabbit when it's hit by a dead-true hunk of lead.

Frank knelt on one knee. The wind picked up. The temperature dropped. It started to snow.

Slade's body vibrated. He tensed. He was ready to kill some more. He thought he'd stopped all of them, but he couldn't be sure. He didn't want to take a stupid chance and walk around checking.

He crawled back to his rock bunker and waited.

The snow came down. Wet, floppy flakes. Slade leveled his rifle-pistol over the rocks. Peterson had been right about his invention. The Goodnight combination pistol-rifle was deadly up close.

Frank waited some more, then he ran from the bunker to the campfire and counted five bodies. Counting the man he'd nailed along the river, that made six. Slade heaved a sigh of relief.

He went around the campfire picking up buffalo chips. He gathered them in a blanket, tied them, and hooked the bundle to his saddle. He guessed he'd need more fire, more warmth, before he made it to Trinidad.

There was always a low, depressing feeling after killing. Frank sat down in the spitting snow. "This should end it for a while," he said to himself as he watched the wafer-size flakes put out his fire.

"I gotta get a move on," Slade said to himself. "Got to make Trinidad."

He knew the odds were good that no one would know him there.

He mounted his slumped roan and rode through the slicing blizzard. Nasty winds swirled around him and whipped snow into marblelike drifts.

Slade's back hurt. It was a tight, gnawing pain. It was like knots had been tied up on his shoulders, along his spine.

The cold night slid through him. Snow spit in his face. Snot hung from his nose. His lips were frozen, but he kept going, pushed the tired roan into the storm until both horse and man were like chunks of ice.

The roan finally gave out. His front legs crumbled. He snorted thick clouds of vapor and fell to his knees. Slade slid down his neck. He rolled the roan on his side. The poor beast was in pain.

"Sorry, boy," Slade whispered. "We're in a hell of a fix."

He helped the horse up, walked him through the blizzard, but then Slade stumbled and fell onto the frozen tundra. He lay sprawled on his belly, hurting as badly as the roan.

The horse dipped his neck and nudged Frank with his nose. Slade grabbed the reins, pulled himself up, and walked into the wind. The snow let up, and Frank made it to the Spanish Peaks near the upper link of Santa Fe Trail.

He walked the horse around big boulders at the base of a mountain, circled to the other side, away from the sideswiping wind, the whirl of the blizzard. He found an overhanging ledge and led the roan under it.

This wasn't the way Slade envisioned his death. "We're gonna make it. We have to make it," Slade mumbled to his horse. "We can't go down like this."

He pulled the blanket of buffalo chips from the horse, but his hands were so numb he couldn't hold it. The chips spilled to the ground.

If he could light the chips there might be a chance. Frank tried to get the box of lucifers out of his pocket. He knelt by the blanket, leaned over, and squeezed the box from his Levi's jacket with both hands. The matches spilled out in front of him.

The roan went down to his knees again.

"Oh, shit!" Slade mumbled. "Hang on, boy, hang on. Don't give up."

But the horse tumbled over on his side and lay snorting, gasping, dying. Slade squatted by the matches. His hands were chunks of ice. He managed to work a rock between his palms. He bent over, raised his arms, then cracked the rock on the box of lucifers. He hacked at them until the rock scratched one into fire. Frank jumped up in time to kick the match into the buffalo chips. The orange flame caught the edge of a pancake-size chip.

Slade smiled. Then the blanket caught fire, and the chips burst into flames. Frank sat down and waved his hands inches above the heat.

He leaned in close and warmed his frozen body. Never had fire felt this good to Slade.

He lay down and cuddled close to the horse, felt what little heat there was from the animal. He wound his arms around the horse's neck. They lay shivering as the blizzard howled around them.

The wind flattened the flames. The snow picked up. The fire died. Slade snuggled closer to the fading heat of the horse.

"Dyin' out here in a blizzard," he whispered. "We're dyin' out here."

Frank slipped into unconsciousness as the last spark of fire was smothered by a snowflake the size of a double-eagle gold coin.

Chapter Fifteen

Cliff Langdon paced the confines of his plush office, his eyes hot with anger.

"How in the hell did it happen?" Langdon yelled.

Seated around his desk were Bat Masterson, the new sheriff, and Marshal Ed Masterson, Under Marshal L. E. Deger, and Judge Lynch.

Langdon stopped, leaned over his desk, and slapped his fat palms on the blotter.

"Well?"

"The woman lawyer," Bat said. "We didn't count on anything like that happening."

"Jesus!" Langdon huffed. "She was a schoolteacher too."

Deger waved his hands. "Hey, Cliff, you're the one told us to let her in. You wanted to make sure that everyone knew Slade was getting a fair break."

The lawmen sat with their Stetsons on their laps. They were honest men and had no idea what had really happened between Frank Slade and Cliff Langdon.

"He got himself a fair trial too," Judge Lynch said.

Bat slid forward on his chair. "A lot of folks are wonderin' about that, Judge, the way you cut off Slade's defense all the time."

"Oh, Christ! Stop bickering!" Langdon shouted.

He slumped into his swivel chair behind the desk, took a deep breath, heaved out his fat belly, and stared intently at the lawmen.

"I'm sorry, gentlemen. Didn't mean to berate you. It's just that hangin' Slade was important to me. He's been spreadin' lies about me, about Dodge City, and then we get him jailed and he escapes."

"I told you not to let anyone near him," Bat interrupted.

Langdon sighed. "None of us would have guessed that the woman would do what she did. But she's dead now. The posse brought word back they found her and Hardin, both with slugs in their backs. I'd guess Slade killed them both. They were both foolish. The lawyer for thinking Slade would carry her on the run, and that damn Hardin, going after Slade alone like that, and him being a fool anyway."

Langdon pulled a long contessa cigar from his humidor, struck a Lucifer under his desk, and puffed the thin cigar into life.

He pushed back in his chair. "It's my fault, gentlemen. I tried to be too fair. We lost him. We had him on the hook, we had him almost in the noose, but we lost him."

"Well, we're not gonna be able to get up another

posse, that's for sure," said Marshal Masterson. "Six men ain't come back. Slade musta killed 'em."

"And it's snowing up in the Jornado. I heard it from some folks comin' up the Santa Fe into Dodge."

"So, we may not see those men until spring," Langdon conjectured.

"Unless it suns up there and thaws. It does that a lot. Gets real cold, then real warm," Bat said.

"Those six men," Langdon said, "they rode the Cimarron river tracking Slade?"

The lawmen nodded.

"So, Slade is headed for high country."

Bat leaned back. "Probably thought he'd have a chance up there." He lit a cheroot and continued. "That's what I'd have done if I was him. Go up to the Raton Pass, up around Trinidad."

"Suggestions?" Langdon said.

"I guess I could go after him," Ed Masterson said.

"I think you boys oughta stay home here in Dodge," Langdon said.

Judge Lynch got up, walked to a shelf of books. He turned and said, "How about Mysterious Dave Mather. I hear he's hangin' out down in Las Vegas, New Mexico. You could send a wire to him, have him ride up to Trinidad, see if he can locate Slade."

"Oh, shit. Come on, you can't trust him," Bat said. "One week he's a lawman, the next he's stealin' women's jewelry."

"Bat's right," Deger said. "Don't get hooked up with Mather. He works both sides."

Langdon puffed his cigar, his eyes shifting from one man to the other. There was no way behind a wild Irish rose he'd hire Mysterious Dave Mather.

Bat leaned on the desk, pressed over toward Langdon, his chin jutting. "I want him, Mr. Langdon. I want Slade."

"I'll bet you do," Langdon said, a smile lifting around his cigar. "But can you handle him?"

"I brought him back to Dodge City, didn't I?"

"With Miss LaRue's help," Langdon was quick to add.

"I want him. I'll go after him."

"You're the sheriff. We need you here," Langdon said.

"Ed can deputize me a U.S. marshal. He can take care of things here."

"All right with you, Ed?" Langdon asked.

Ed Masterson shrugged his shoulders. "I reckon Bat hasn't had his fill of newspaper stories about him yet. Sure, I'll deputize him."

"Then it's settled," Bat said, relaxing back into his chair. "I'll bring Slade back again."

Langdon stood up and dismissed the men. He had no illusions about Bat Masterson. If Bat wanted to make a name and go after Slade, that was fine with him.

"Bat," he called.

Masterson turned at the door.

"Slade has sent me the badge of every marshal we've put on him."

"Not this time," Bat said, then strode through the door.

Judge Lynch lingered after the other men had left. He put his black hat on, turned, and said, "Cliff, you might just want to let this thing go. Especially if you hanker to be governor, as I know you do. Slade's becoming some kind of folk hero."

"Kansas is the center of commerce. The rest of the country needs what we have here. Cattle. Dead meat. And that's how I see Frank Slade. Dead meat. And don't worry, Judge. I'll be governor."

The judge twisted his head to one side, his eyebrow raised. "Don't get obsessed with this, Cliff. It could hurt you."

"I'll keep that in mind, Judge. Thank you."

The judge left and Langdon waddled to the door and called his secretary. "Wanda, come in here a minute."

Wanda walked behind him to his desk. She wore a blue and white frock. Her brown hair flowed lazily from her head. She was thirty-five, educated, and she worked hard for Cliff Langdon. She knew the old banker was going to be the next governor of Kansas, then perhaps move on to the U.S. Senate, maybe even be president, and she wanted some of the action.

Langdon smiled. "Did you see my daughter off to college in California?"

"Yes, sir. I took Lucy to the train. She's on her way."

"Fine. And how are folks reacting to what happened with Frank Slade?"

"They are disappointed there was no hanging, sir."

"I see."

"But they know you are doing your best. They know who made Kansas happen, they know you are a good man, sir, that you were responsible for making Dodge City and Kansas what it is, what it has become."

"And you think they'll vote for me . . . if I run for governor?"

"Without a doubt, sir. You've brought employment to this area. You had a vision. You saw the potential."

"They're not sympathetic with Frank Slade?"

"No, sir. No way."

"Good, good. I want you to keep a pulse on things with the common folk. I want to know what they're thinking. I want to make sure they like Cliff Langdon."

"Oh, indeed, sir. That's a simple assignment."

Langdon got off his chair, swiggled around his desk. Wanda got up. Cliff opened his arms. She pressed into him. He kissed her, and she undulated against the aging banker.

Langdon lifted her dress, slid it up in ruffles on Wanda's generous hips. He slid his hand between her legs. "Did you check out Niles Caldwell for me, Wanda?" he whispered.

"Mmmm," Wanda mumbled, flicking out her tongue, sloshing it around Langdon's ear.

"And what did you find out, dear?"

"He's mean. He's young, about Slade's age. He gunned down six men in Ellsworth last month. It was ruled self-defense. Ooooohh, Cliff, that feels good."

She was taller than Langdon. He looked up into her face. She radiated a pristine beauty. "Six men in Ellsworth?" he whispered.

"They said—and I quote here, sir—that Caldwell is reckless and as fast with a gun as a trout hitting a hook."

"Sounds interesting," Langdon said.

"He's over in Abilene right now. They say he doesn't know what fear is, sir. He'd be a good bet if you're thinking what I think you're thinking."

Langdon kept working his hands around on Wanda's red bloomers. "You think he's our man, Wanda?"

"If I wanted Frank Slade dead, if I wanted justice to be done, I'd hire Niles Caldwell," Wanda said.

"Get word to him, Wanda. I want him in Dodge City

within forty-eight hours. Now, should we retire to the couch over there?''

"I'd love to, sir, but your wife is due in a few minutes. You're scheduled to escort her to the pie social at the church this afternoon.''

"I forgot about that, Wanda. I simply forgot about that. What would I do without you?''

Wanda dropped her dress, patted it in place, and smiled. "I'm always at your service, sir. I'll have Niles Caldwell in your office in forty-eight hours.''

"Good, Wanda. I wish I could stay with you. I hate pie socials.''

"Oh, but you must go, Mr. Langdon. It will be good for your campaign when you launch it. You have so much to offer, and as you often say, the end justifies the means. Think of it that way.''

Langdon had always thought of life that way. That's why he'd had Frank Slade's mom and dad killed and taken their land. He'd had a vision for Kansas, and he wasn't about to let some poor farmers stand in the way of progress.

"Leave the door open, Wanda," he said, relighting his long cigar.

Wanda left and Langdon waddled around his desk and sat down. He leaned back to think. *What the hell was he to do about Frank Slade?*

Slade was the only link to Langdon's past, his illegal land grab. All the killing and stealing. It had not been pretty. But his plan had worked and that's all that mattered to Cliff Langdon. The ends did justify the means as Wanda had said, and hadn't the means been good for Kansas? Wasn't Dodge City on the move, wasn't the state prosperous?

Still, those acts of ruthlessness were a part of Langdon's life, no matter how much he lied about it or protected himself. His black past hung over him in the shadow of Frank Slade.

Langdon got up, paced his office, looked out the window, and saw Bat Masterson ride west down Front Street.

Cliff Langdon smiled. If Bat could bring Slade back by himself he'd secure his legend, and Cliff Langdon would be free of his past. But if Masterson couldn't get the job done, there was Niles Caldwell.

Chapter Sixteen

S lade felt the warmth of a fire and heard voices before he was fully awake. It was as if he'd come back from death. Had the rest of the posse caught up with him? Was he a prisoner again? Would the Dodge City hanging noose be tugging on his neck?

Someone threw a chip in the fire. The flames crackled and spit.

The conversation was led by a man with a stern, demanding voice. "The storm will break soon," he said. "We must pray. God is our guidance. I am God's inspiration. God has instructed us to stay here in the caves, then move west. *Pray!* All of you! Silence, while God speaks to me."

Caves?

Slade wondered if he might be in the caves on Simpson's Rest above Trinidad. He also wondered who the hell he was with.

The fire spritzed. The wind howled outside. Slade opened his eyes and waited while they focused on jagged rock around him. He turned his head slightly, quietly, and saw three men and four women on their knees around a fire.

They were dressed in severe religious garb—the men in black, the women in high-top gray dresses with white bonnets. The leader, a tall, thin man, stood up. He lifted his face upward and raised his arms in a stiff V. His fingers twitched.

"God speaks through me!" he shouted. "God speaks!"

A chorus of "amens" echoed through the cave.

"He's testing us. God tests our determination. This storm is a test of our will, our love."

"Amen!"

"God tells me to keep going, take my wives and disciples farther west. We're not through. This is not the place. It's farther west. That's where we will start our new church. I see it! God is showing me the place. It's beautiful. It's sacred. This is where the Church of the Pure Inspiration will prosper. God speaks through me. I shall have ten offspring from each wife. We will multiply. We will grow."

"Amen!"

"Praise be to God!"

Slade watched the strange ceremony. His stomach grumbled. His body ached.

"Do you hear me? God has spoken!" the leader yelled, then fell back to his knees. "Do you hear?"

"Yes, Malachi," the group chanted.

"Amen, my children," Malachi whispered.

Slade tried to get up from the rock floor, but he fell with a thud.

"Ah, our friend is back among the living. See? God answered our prayers. He has a role for this young man. We need more men. He will be a disciple. He will help us grow."

A young woman came to Slade. She knelt beside him and held a cup of steaming broth to his lips. Slade sipped and warmed to the slow melt of the liquid through his chest and down into his belly.

"Where am I?" Slade whispered.

Malachi stood over Frank. His eyes had a sinister glow that was reflected by the flames of the fire.

"In a cluster of caves, my boy, somewhere in Colorado."

"Simpson's Rest," Slade mumbled.

"What, lad?"

"The caves. This is called Simpson's Rest. We're right above Trinidad."

"We want no association with cities," Malachi said. "We will wait out the storm, then head to our new home farther west."

The girl offered more broth. Slade sipped.

"My guns, saddlebags?" he asked.

"We have them," Malachi answered.

Frank took Malachi's terse remark to mean that they would keep them too. He managed a sitting position. A quick spell of dizziness flooded his head.

"Soon as I get my strength I'll be movin' on," Frank whispered.

"Oh, no, my boy, God has a plan for you. You'll stay with us. Help us build our church."

Frank lay back. No use arguing. He was too weak.

"Feed him, Amanda," Malachi ordered.

The girl got up, went to the fire, and Frank heard a slab of meat hit a skillet. It sizzled and the smell of fresh-cooked venison filled the cave.

"We are caught in a blizzard," Malachi said, still standing over Slade, peering down at him. "We found you dying, your horse dead. We brought you here to these caves with us. It was God's will. You must thank God for your good fortune."

Slade could tell from the look on Malachi's face and the way he talked that he was crazy.

"We will wait out the storm, the melting, then we will travel west, and you'll go with us. I will teach you the Word. You will be a good disciple."

Oh, shit, Frank thought. He couldn't have been saved by some nice normal folks headed down the Santa Fe Trail. No, he had to end up with a religious fanatic who wanted to make him part of his cult. Slade nodded to Malachi to appease him, then leaned back and sat against the cave. He looked out the opening into a wall of swirling snow.

Amanda brought him a tin plate of meat and parched corn. Frank ate slowly, savoring the taste of the food. He figured if he could belt down a couple of shots of whiskey his strength would return a lot sooner. But he knew better than to ask.

Slade ate and thought things over. He'd wait, find a way to escape. But for now he was trapped with a madman and his band of followers.

Chapter Seventeen

The next two days Slade rested and listened closely. He inspected as much of the cave as he could from his vantage. The group had their horses in the cave, toward the back by an underground stream. He guessed their wagons were outside, in the blizzard, at the base of the mountain.

Frank pieced together a story from the scraps of conversation around the fire. The four women were married to Malachi. The two men were followers. They had broken off from the Amana Colony in Iowa.

The Amana group was widely known because of their innovative farming methods. They had left Germany because a rift had developed in the Lutheran Church over ritual.

They were influenced by scholars who had studied mysticism and pietism. They came to believe that God communicates to his followers through an inspired individual, just as he did in biblical stories.

Malachi kept referring to himself as a *Werkzeug*, an instrument of God.

In 1842, the group of Lutheran dissidents had come to America and purchased land in the Seneca Indian Reservation near Buffalo, New York.

They'd established a communal system, but because Buffalo experienced explosive growth, and to get away from the worldly influence of the city, the Amana group had moved west and bought eighteen thousand acres in east central Iowa. They'd built a village and chosen the name *Amana*, which meant to "remain true," from the Song of Solomon in the Bible.

Malachi and his followers read the Bible by the campfire, constantly stoking the flames with chips from gunnysacks. At night they prayed.

Slade's strength returned, and he was able to walk the cave. He stood at the mouth and watched the storm whirl around the ledge outside.

Malachi approached him. "You'll pray with us now, Mr. Slade."

Frank turned and faced him. "You do your own praying. I'm leaving as soon as the storm stops."

Malachi stiffened as if he'd been hit by an arrow. His glassy eyes stared at Frank. "I said, 'You'll pray with us now.' You'll pray with us and study the Word. You'll do as I say, Mr. Slade."

"Look," Frank said, "you may have these folks fooled, but I'm on to you. I know what you have planned for me. You need a worker, two hands, muscles. I want no part of your scheme."

"Carl! Adam!" Malachi yelled.

Malachi's two followers rushed to his side. They were big. Their faces carried a stupid, empty look.

Malachi grinned. "Mr. Slade is reluctant to join our church. He must be punished."

Carl hunkered over Slade. He was like a bear and several inches taller than Frank's lean six-three frame. His black suit was too small, and his gangly arms hung apelike out of the sleeves of his coat, which pulled halfway up on his arms. He raised a rifle and pointed it at Frank.

Adam, a short, squat man, pushed Slade back into the interior of the cave.

Slade let go with a hard right and sent Adam sprawling. Carl swung his rifle and butted Frank on the neck. Slade toppled. Malachi produced a whip and cracked it with a vicious snap at Frank's back.

Carl cocked the rifle and pointed it at Slade's head. Malachi grinned insanely, twirled the whip, and snaked it with a loud snap against Frank's shoulders.

Adam got up. He produced a rope and tied Slade's wrists. The men dragged Frank back to his place by the fire, then tied his ankles.

"You'll pray with us now," Malachi said.

"Fuck you, you bastard!" Frank shouted, loud enough for the prissy women to hear.

Malachi lashed the whip, caught Slade on the left shoulder with a loud crack. Then he gathered his clan. The women dipped to their knees, bonnets tipped forward.

Malachi stood over them in the glow of the fire. Carl and Adam stood across from Malachi where they could see Slade.

"God speaks," said Malachi. "I hear the rumble. I

feel the thunder. This man, Slade, is full of the devil. He must be punished. Satan must be exorcised from his body, from his soul.''

''Amen, amen.''

''He gives us no thanks for saving his life. But we will teach him. We will instruct him. *Amana! Amana! Amana!*''

''*Faith! Faith! Faith!*'' the group chanted.

''Aw, shit! Just kill me! I been through too much to put up with this crap!'' Slade yelled.

Malachi stretched his arms outward, fingers twitching, and shouted, ''Children, children, believers of the Pure Inspiration! We are being tested again! Satan has sent us an evil one! We must conquer him, redeem him, and save his soul!''

Malachi turned and twirled his whip, smacked it against Slade's back. Pain shot through Frank. He sat helplessly and looked over at the women. They were on their knees, hands steepled. They looked several years apart in age, from forty down to the youngest one, Amanda, the one who'd fed him broth. She had to be in her late teens.

''Don't you women see what this freak is trying to do?'' Frank yelled. ''Don't you realize what's happening here? How can *all* you women be his wife?''

Whack!

The whip cut into Slade's back. Malachi hit him again and again until Frank passed out.

Deep in the night the fire died down to hot coals. Slade stirred. His back hurt. The rope on his wrists and ankles was godawful tight, but it was nothing compared to the weeks in irons he'd suffered through in Dodge City.

He lay curled against the cave wall. The wind screamed outside. He saw Amanda crawling to him. He looked for Carl and Adam. They were both asleep.

"You have to help us, Mr. Slade," Amanda whispered. "He just took us. He stole us from Amana. He and the other men. Do you understand?"

"In my boot, the right one, there's a knife. Slip it out and cut me loose," Frank said softly.

Amanda found Slade's Eagle knife. She pulled the blade from his boot and slit the rope on his wrists. Frank looked down into her young face. The poor girl was terrified.

He wanted to grab her, tell her everything would be okay, that he himself was in trouble. Then his mind was rattled by a quick memory of Abby, how her blood had trickled into his caressing hands as they made love.

Frank took the Eagle knife from Amanda and cut his legs loose. He put the knife back in his boot and whispered, "Where are my possibles?"

"Over by Carl," Amanda said.

Slade crawled on his belly toward Carl. He had to smile at the group's inexperience in taking and keeping him prisoner, but they had no idea, of course, they had tied up the infamous Frank Slade.

Amanda slid back to the other women, slipped under her blanket, and pulled it around her chin.

Slade bellied like a low cloud across the cave to Carl. He saw his Goodnight Winchester leaning against the wall next to Carl's Henry repeater.

Carl snored offensively. Slade took a good look at the man. His snorts lifted the whiskers on his upper lip as he exhaled.

Frank grabbed his gun, cocked it, and nudged Carl.

The ugly man leapt from the floor. His bulky weight slammed into Slade. Frank fell on his ass. Carl lunged in a wild belly flop. Slade twisted and Carl smashed to the rock surface of the cave. Frank lifted to one knee and leveled his Goodnight at Carl.

Carl kicked his leg into the barrel of the gun. The Goodnight flew out of Slade's hands. Frank pulled his Eagle knife. Carl came off the floor hunched, charging like a bull.

Slade sliced the knife into Carl's belly. The big man gasped. His mouth came unhinged. He groaned and his eyes looked as though they might spit from his head.

He fell beside Frank in a soft pile of flesh.

The racket had awakened Adam. He jumped from his blanket, cocked his rifle, and pumped two shots at Slade. Frank rolled to the right, the left, and came up with an overhanded toss, twirling the Eagle knife in a bloody cartwheel into the boy's chest.

Adam, curled, dipped to his knees, and looked up at Slade. He gulped, then died.

Slade grabbed his gun.

Malachi charged him, an ax waving wildly from his hand.

"Drop it or you're dead!" Frank yelled.

"The devil be damned!" Malachi shouted.

The women woke from their sleep and knelt in prayer.

"Your *god be damned*!" Slade yelled back.

Malachi backed off. "We saved you. You'd be dead if we hadn't been gracious and taken you in with us."

"I know what you had planned for me, old man . . . same as you had planned for all the others. You'd make me your slave."

"God will punish you for this. You'll burn in hell."

"Can it, you old fart!" Slade growled. "You're the one who'll fry in hell . . . if there is such a place. You kidnapped these women. Now *you* pray!"

Malachi stood stiffly.

"On your knees!" Slade yelled.

The women looked up at the scene unfolding by the fire.

"I'll give you five seconds," Slade said.

Malachi smirked at Frank and refused to go down. Frank moved closer, pushed the barrel of the Goodnight into Malachi's chest.

God's instrument folded to his knees.

"Pray!" Frank yelled. "Let's see your god save you now, because I don't think you have the same god as the rest of us folks."

Malachi tilted his face, looked up at Frank with hate in his crazy eyes.

"I said, 'Pray!' " Slade shouted.

Malachi raised his arms in a wide V, his fingers wiggling.

"God is speaking to me!" Malachi said.

Slade backed off two steps. He lifted the Goodnight. "God is speaking to me too, Malachi," Frank said. "He's saying, 'Good night, Malachi.' " Slade triggered off two shots into the sick religious leader. Malachi slammed forward, his head banging to the cave floor.

There was a death-matching silence from the women, then jubilation. Slade walked to the cave's opening. The storm had calmed. The snow had stopped. Frank turned and looked back at the dead and the living.

"I love life!" he hollered.

Chapter Eighteen

The next morning Slade stood at the mouth of the cave. He reckoned he and the women were stranded on the lower ledges of Simpson's Rest. The sun was already melting the huge drifts on the ledges. Frank kept to himself for the next two days. The women prayed and stayed away from him too.

On the third day after the blizzard, Slade took one of their spades and his possibles in a roll, and promised the women he would send someone back for them when he got to Trinidad.

"Oh, no, that won't be necessary," the older woman said. "We'll wait until the snow melts, then we'll make our way back to Iowa, back to the colony in Amana where we lived."

"That'll be tough going this time of year," Slade warned.

"It's what we decided. That's where we belong."

Frank nodded and started to leave.

"And thanks, Mr. Slade, for helping us. You will always be in our prayers."

Slade tipped his hat and slipped out onto the ledge. He started shoveling his way through the snow, curving downward, cutting a tunnel toward flat land. He worked most of the day. He passed some other people in caves, still waiting out the thaw.

It was late afternoon when the skies darkened, the wind whipped up, the temperature dropped, and it started snowing again.

Slade shoveled faster, but the snow piled up. Visibility dropped to zero. He came to a cave and crawled in. The mouth gave way to a large room with a fire. An old man in sheepskin, with an Abe Lincoln hat perched on his head, sat across the fire from a young woman in a thick buffalo coat.

"You headed into Trinidad?" the girl asked.

"Tryin' to," Frank said, his lips barely moving they were so cold.

"Or maybe running from somethin'?" the old man said, giving Slade a wizened smile.

"Can I share your fire?" Frank mumbled.

"Why, sure, come right on in," the old man said. "This here's Sue O'Riley, and I'm Professor Winfield Scott. We're a team."

The girl looked up at Frank and grinned. "And you're Frank Slade," she said.

Her black hair shone on her forehead under the brim of a floppy hat. Her face reflected back to Slade in the glow of the fire. She had high, proud cheeks, a jutting chin, brown eyes, and thick lips.

"Never heard of him," Slade said, sitting down across from Sue and Professor Scott.

"It's okay, lad, we recognized you. We were in Dodge City during your trial."

Slade reached for his gun, but his fingers were numb. He couldn't clutch the handle of his Colt.

The old man waved his arms. "No need for that, Mr. Slade. We won't turn you in. Quite the contrary. We stay as far away from the law as we can. Seems like when we leave town they have questions about our marketing and selling program."

"We got a medicine show," said Sue O'Riley.

"Fact is, the law is generally after us by the time we've left town, but then we're ahead of them."

"Before they find out we screwed 'em," Sue added.

The girl handed a cup of hot coffee to Slade. The tin cup warmed his hands. He sipped slowly.

The professor lifted a jug of whiskey and slugged down a big gulp. He wiped his mouth on the sleeve of his sheepskin coat. "No, sir," he said. "We wouldn't turn you in."

Sue took the jug from the professor and handed it to Frank. "He's right, Slade. We admire you," she said, her voice warm as the steaming coffee spilled through his insides.

"A medicine show?" Frank said, taking the whiskey. He lifted the jug with both frozen hands, found his mouth, and poured the rotgut into his throat.

Sue and the professor watched. Frank felt a stiff jolt. The booze was as tough as paint, but it made him feel better.

"Yes, a medicine show," the professor said. "Suzy here dances, does a nice eye-catching routine, gets real sexy, draws the men, then I sell the product. Dr. Scott's Enigmatic Elixir, a potent formula for those men who need a little *lift* in their life, if you get my drift.''

Slade nodded. ''Did you see any men on your way here?'' he asked.

The professor rubbed his whiskers. ''Only thing we saw was all those bodies back up the Santa Fe. You blew the holy shit out of those boys. Did you use explosives?''

''Can't remember,'' Slade whispered, then leaned back against a rock.

''We have a wagon just below the cave, down on the flat, and we got the mules warm here in the cave, down the tunnel there where the stream flows. Soon as the snow lets up we're headed for Trinidad. You could go in with us.''

''Yeah,'' Sue said. ''Soon as the blizzard stops there'll be supply trains comin' down the Santa Fe. You don't want to let 'em see you.''

Slade handed the jug back to the professor, then stuck his hands over the fire, wiggling his fingers. He leaned closer and felt his circulation throbbing back into his body.

''These caves are full of people waiting out the storm,'' the professor said.

Slade wasn't about to tell them about his experience several rims above them, how he'd killed three men and left four women with wild hopes of returning to Iowa.

''You had quite an ordeal, lad, back there in Dodge City,'' the professor said.

Slade whispered, ''People never cease to disappoint you.''

''Ah yes. Well put, my boy.''

"What the hell does that mean?" Sue asked.

"Mr. Slade is waxing philosophical, my pet," said the professor. "He means that one is open to people, has high hopes about them, then they let you down. Right, Slade?"

Slade looked up at the old man.

"Somethin' like that," he said.

"Oh, indeed," the professor grumbled. "People do disappoint you. Suzanne here and I had an appalling experience back in Iowa City where I was professing."

"Yeah, they kicked him out of the university," Sue put in.

"Our halls of academia, Mr. Slade, have been infiltrated by cretins."

Sue grinned. "Yeah, and he was kicked out of William and Mary before Iowa."

"I was sacked," said the professor, lifting the whiskey jug. His Adam's apple bobbed as he gulped.

"They sacked him at the University of Iowa because he was puttin' the make on me," Sue O'Riley said.

"That's not true, my dove, and you know it. But our association did rile some people. Such gossip, all the conjecture, and there was nothing to it, Mr. Slade."

Frank considered their confessions, then stated, "So, you two were lovers, and they kicked you out of Iowa City."

"No, no!" the professor squeaked. "I've never touched the young tart."

"But he wanted to," Sue said.

The professor looked at her. "Well, who wouldn't, my sweet nymph?"

"You sure do," she argued.

"You said you wanted to explore the world, you wanted to travel, darling."

"I never thought it would be like this, though, up here in the middle of a goddamn blizzard, stuck in a cave."

The professor turned to Slade for consultation. "Ask her how much money she's made since we left Iowa City, sir."

Slade cuddled the tin cup of coffee. He looked at Sue. "How much money have you made since you left Iowa City?"

"A lot, but—"

The professor jumped up. "There are no *buts*! She's getting rich. Tell him, go ahead, tell Mr. Slade," the professor barked, wagging a finger at Sue O'Riley.

Slade wished he could ditch both of them, get on with his escape from Dodge City, but he was stuck. He knew it. They knew it.

The professor turned stoically to Sue. "You may leave me, my little minx, any time you feel like it. Any time you're not happy."

Sue took off her hat, ran her right hand through her thick black hair. "Naw," she sighed. "It's okay."

"It's okay. Did you hear that, Slade? The sweet strumpet is making more money than she ever thought possible! See how much grief she gives me?"

"Well, tough shit!" Sue hissed.

"Stuff it, both of you," Slade grumbled. "A deal's a deal."

"See, see, my little minx . . . Mr. Slade is right. He understands. In fact, I think Slade's got some education, right, Slade?"

"Only through grade seven. I had to work on my folks' farm. But I read a lot."

"Of course you do. Of course you do," the professor puffed, rising from his perch again. He paced the fire. "That's how one learns."

Slade ached. His body wanted to fold up after all the shoveling he'd done, and he didn't feel like sitting in the mountains overlooking Trinidad with two people who argued all the time.

"I'll just warm up some more, then I'll be on my way," Frank said, "soon as the blizzard stops."

The professor took another drink. "You can ride down with us in our wagon."

"I'd be obliged," said Slade.

The professor passed the jug to Slade. "It may not be too long. It can turn warm in this part of the country just as easy as it gets cold. The sun will come out. The snow will melt, then two or three days later you might see another blizzard."

Slade wiped the top of the jug and took another shot. It was awful whiskey, but it had the same effect as Evan Williams, Sweet Home, or Jim Beam. A good solid jolt.

The professor pitched several cow chips into the flames. "One good thing about following the Santa Fe Trail," he said, smiling. "There's lots of shit to burn."

The fire popped. Slade checked things out. They were at the opening of the cave on a rock ledge in front of an overhanging cliff. The wind swirled and howled at the mouth of the cave.

Slade, Sue, and the professor kept warm around the rock fireplace, and the professor fed the fire with chips from a gunnysack.

Frank dozed and listened to the professor's unending drivel of information, a blatant intellectual show, while his young student treated him with indifference and argued back.

Slade lost track of the hours. The blizzard stopped twice, but then whipped up again. The rock floor of the cave made an uncomfortable bed for his tired body. His back had tightened up from the lashing he'd taken from Malachi. It was sore and tender.

The professor constantly baited him. "Tell us about your life, Slade."

"Nothin' to tell."

The old man smiled. "We know better than that. You drew a big crowd to Dodge for your hangin'."

"Yeah, and the professor and I made a pile of dough off those folks too," said Sue O'Riley.

"You make us sound like mercenary scoundrels, Suzanne," the professor protested.

"Oh, God, Professor, leave Slade alone. He doesn't wanna talk about his life. Can't you see that? Besides, you know all about it."

"Yes, of course. You're right, my little whippet. Please forgive me, Slade."

In order to shut the professor off, Frank asked him for a book. "Got anything to read?"

"Always keep my Descartes with me."

"Day . . . who?" Slade asked.

"Rene Descartes. He was a French philosopher," Sue said.

The professor smiled. "A man of great importance, great influence on the intellectual movement. Lived back in the sixteen hundreds."

The professor pulled a worn book from his valise and handed it to Slade. "Descartes' *Cogito Ergo Sum* means 'I think, therefore I am.' "

"Yeah, what a big breakthrough for the world. The guy found out he could think, then he realized he was alive," Sue said. "Big deal."

Slade didn't care, he just wanted to get his nose into the book so he could avoid any more bickering and talking. He read slowly and didn't understand much of what Descartes was saying, but he was able to find something about doubt, that a man should doubt everything. Slade liked that philosophy.

He read by the fire until Sue and the professor fell asleep. Frank lay back too, pulled an Indian blanket over his tired body, and closed his eyes.

He was in deep sleep when Sue O'Riley shook him awake. She leaned down close and whispered, "Listen, if we're gonna do it, we gotta hurry."

She was wrapped in a black blanket. Her dark hair was combed out. She had put on some fine-smelling perfume.

Sue's lips tasted fresh. Her tongue slushed into Slade's mouth. She opened the blanket, and it fell down her back, then to her feet.

Frank hooked his arms around her, his rough fingers sliding across the smooth glacierlike shoulders, down her naked back, then up again, along her ribbed spine.

Sue's hand groped between Slade's legs. She found his massive erection. Her fingers inspected the length of Frank's hardness.

Slade's hands worked up and down her back. She was tiny and fragile. He nibbled her tongue and slid his hands around in front of her and held her soft breasts on his palms, his fingers scratching the areolas. Sue loosened Slade's fly, slowly flicking the buttons out of their holes with her thumb. She flapped the jeans open and gripped Frank's cock.

Sue lifted herself on one leg, hooked her knee to the rock floor of the cave on the other side of Slade, and straddled him. Her hand clutched his hardness. She humped up and screwed down slowly.

"Awww, shit, Slade," she whispered.

Frank clapped his hands to her thin hips. Sue hung her head over him. Her hair sprayed his face like a waterfall.

She pushed down on Slade, took him into her soft sheath.

Frank spiked upward.

Sue stiffened. Her voice sizzled like the fire beside them. "Slade! God, Slade!" she whispered.

She rocked up and down, back and forth. Her palms were flat on Slade's shoulders. She peered down into his handsome face.

Slade gave thanks to Lady Fortune's spinning wheel for a prize like Sue O'Riley, a beautiful gem in the rugged ruts of life.

Sue pushed forward and bounced slowly on top of Slade, then bent over and kissed him. Frank bit her lips, nibbled them, and sucked them into his mouth.

Sue broke the kiss and sat back up on Slade, bucked him like a bronc rider, her fine, young body rippling. Frank worked with her, lifted his butt off the blanket and pushed deeper up into Sue's tightness.

"Jesus, that's good, Slade," she huffed, then bent down again close to Frank's face. Her lips were inches from his. She licked out her tongue, then said, "Know what I think?"

"No, tell me, Sue."

"That Descartes, the guy the professor was talkin' about?"

"Yeah?" Slade said, his voice unsure.

Sue rolled slowly, stopped and kissed Slade, and purred into his ear as she started undulating again. "That business about 'I think, therefore I am'?"

"Mmm, mmm," Slade mumbled.

Sue licked Frank's chin. Her hips corkscrewed slowly. "That's not such a breakthrough," she whispered. "I could go him one better."

"How's that, Sue?" Slade asked, swiveling off the rock shelf.

"If it was me I woulda said, 'I *fuck*, therefore I am.' "

Slade shuddered and released. Sue stiffened. Her body shook with his. An orange lick of fire danced beside them like a torch burning a hole in the night.

Sue slumped on top of Slade, then she slowly rolled off and wrapped herself in the black blanket. She turned to Frank. "I got somethin' to talk over with you," she whispered. "Somethin' we got in common."

Slade was about to ask what might that be when the professor stirred and rolled over. Sue crawled quickly away to her own makeshift bed.

Slade wondered what in the name of Fortune he could have in common with Sue O'Riley.

Chapter Nineteen

The next morning Sue fried venison in a skillet. The blizzard was letting up. Slade stood at the mouth of the cave.

The professor got up and walked to Frank's side. "It's giving out," he said.

A few minutes later, as if the old faker had been omniscient, the snow stopped. The sun squinted through and steamed off a soggy layer of fog.

"Invigorating rays, I must say," said the professor, lifting his old face to the sun. Then he turned back to Sue at the fire. "You see, my dear, the higher you are up here the hotter the sun."

He looked at Slade and winked. "The cranky lass learns so much from me."

Slade shrugged.

"Yes indeed. This is a moderate climate in all seasons in this part of the country. Oh, it can snow and storm, but then the sun comes out and melts it all down. We'll be leaving for Trinidad soon.''

The venison steaks smelled good to Slade. He was about to leave the professor and join Sue at the fire, when the professor said, ''Look, over there. Fisher's Peak, just across the way. The clouds are breaking up.''

Slade looked out. The clouds shrouding Fisher's Peak lifted, revealing the staircase steps at the top. The peak was an incredible volcanic landmark that jutted nearly ten thousand feet into the sky.

To the west Slade saw the Sangre de Cristo Mountains, the Mountains of Christ.

Then the clouds split and Trinidad was visible below in a beautiful valley along the front range of the Rocky Mountains.

Slade took several deep breaths, sucked in the thin, fresh air, and went back into the cave. He sat down beside Sue. ''Smells mighty good,'' he said.

The professor slid in across from him. ''Indians lived here, up from Mexico. You can see the drawings on these cave walls. But even before the Indians, thousands of years ago, there were living creatures inhabiting this area. Yes indeed. They recently discovered the longest single trail of dinosaur tracks in the world just southeast of here.''

''Oh, for Jesus H. Christ's sake, will you knock it off for a while, professor?'' Sue snapped.

''Oh, of course, my sweet little hussy. We don't want to bother your pretty head with such mundane information,'' the professor said, smiling.

''And stop calling me all those names. I'm tired of it. And I'm tired of all your goddamn lectures too.''

The professor turned to Slade. "She can be a very egregious young lady when she wants to be."

"I thought what you said was interesting, Professor," Slade said. "How do you know all that information?"

"Sir, please. I am an anthropologist, a historian. I have a doctorate in my field."

"He knows a lot of shit, but he gets boring," Sue O'Riley said, turning the venison in the skillet. Her thick buffalo coat opened. She had on a baggy wool sweater.

"We know about Trinidad because it was settled so long ago by the Mexicans," the professor said.

Slade asked, "What were they doin' up here?"

"Looking for new farmland. But after the Civil War Trinidad became a cattle town, and the largest cattle firms in the West settled out here. But as I understand it, from some research I did for a paper before I was so appallingly sacked by the University of Iowa, the Santa Fe Railroad has already extended track to Trinidad because they've discovered coal down there now."

"Can't you just lay off for a while?" Sue barked. She turned to Slade. "Every time we've gone through a patch of land he's had to do a lecture on it."

The professor appealed to Slade. "One day she'll thank me, Slade. She'll see how all this is history in the making."

Slade nodded.

Sue turned the steaks again.

"For example," the professor continued, "in a couple years the railroad will lay tracks all the way to Santa Fe. Well, it's easy to see when that happens the Santa Fe Trail will become nothing but a name in history books."

Sue O'Riley fished the steaks out of the skillet, took

a knife, cut them into pieces, and passed plates around. "Let's eat, then dig the wagon out and get the shit out of this cave."

The professor swiveled his head, his wrinkled neck stretching. He looked at Sue with a broad smile. "I believe the lovely whippet has blasted my narrative with a sweet bullet of logic, Slade."

Slade hoped so. He was ready to get out of the caves too, ready to move on, stay ahead of his trackers.

Chapter Twenty

Sue worked with the hand spade. Slade crunched into the snow around the wagon with a shovel, and the professor axed away the ice near the wheels.

The sun was hot now, spraying an Indian summer on the Colorado-New Mexico border. The professor hooked up the mules.

The wagon lifted and started them along a trail down into the valley toward Trinidad.

They got stuck a mile down.

Slade slid from the back of the wagon, walked around front. The professor and Sue leaned to the right, looked back at him.

"Didn't see that dip," the professor said.

"Well, shit! We're in the mud now," Sue huffed, slipping off her seat, jumping to the ground. "It's the back wheels."

The professor worked the mules. Slade and Sue dug around the wheels, then pushed. The wagon heaved up over the slippery wash.

They hit the flatland between the mountains and followed a muddy trail next to the Purgatoire in as far as Cedar Street on the outskirts of Trinidad.

Slade jumped off the wagon. He walked to the front with his possibles. "This is where I get off," he yelled.

"Now wait just a damn minute!" Sue O'Riley yelled. "I got somethin' to talk over with you, Slade."

"I'll be in town for a while," Frank said.

"What would that be, my dove?" the professor asked. "What do you have to discuss with Mr. Slade?"

"None of your business, Professor, and if you had just shut up for a minute, maybe I could have discussed it with Slade." She looked down at Frank. "You'll want to know what I have to say."

"If it's important you'll find me," Frank said, then waved at them and started down Cedar Street into Trinidad.

He was relieved to be rid of the professor and Sue O'Riley, and he was eager to plot his next move.

Sue O'Riley held the reins to the mules. She lifted one hand and shoved up her middle finger.

"Hey, Slade!" she called.

Slade turned and saw her lewd sign.

He shook his head, shrugged, and hauled his possibles down the street.

He walked past the Baca House, a two-story territorial adobe. The famous house had belonged to Don Feline Baca, who'd settled Trinidad with his family back in the early 1860s. Baca had made his money in sheep.

Slade admired the beautiful mid-Victorian architecture. The *corrillera* sat behind the house and had at one time housed the farmhands and sheepherders who worked for Baca.

Slade carried his possibles slung over his shoulders. He found Main Street and ambled down the brick road, stepped up to the board sidewalk, and passed the Bloom Cattle Company. Then he walked past Thatcher and Brothers, past the Matado Land and Cattle Company, all imposing structures that spread a shadow of wealth over the narrow street.

Frank felt good being alone again. More secure. Ready for anything. Maybe it was the way his life had shaped up, but he couldn't take too much of people.

Slade walked past stone buildings that had been constructed with the help of the Trinidad Brick Works north of town. Its imprint was carved on the sides of the structures. He passed the First National Bank, the Trinidad Opera House, and came to the Trinidad Hotel and Saloon. He pulled his possibles tighter across his shoulders and walked in.

The check-in counter was new, a solid oak structure with a horseshoe curve. A young man in a gray three-piece suit greeted Slade.

"A room, a bed, some sleep, I assume."

Slade smirked. "I assume," he said.

Frank dropped his saddlebags and roll, leaned on the counter, his face scraggly with a black beard, his lean frame thinner than usual, tired. Yes, he needed a room, a bed, and some sleep.

"A suite, perhaps?" the clerk asked.

Slade pushed in closer, admonishing the young clerk with his bright green eyes. "Now, tell me, asshole, do I look like a man who wants a suite?"

"Of course not, sir. You want a room on the second floor."

"That would be overlooking the street?"

"Yes, two-eighteen."

"Where I have a good view?"

"Certainly." •

"I'll take it, then. And bring me a bottle of whiskey and some cheroots."

"That'll be two dollars for the room, two bits for the whiskey, and two bits for good cheroots."

"I don't want two-bit whiskey. You got any Sweet Home?"

"Yes, sir."

"Then bring me a bottle of Sweet Home."

Slade hauled his bags up to two-eighteen, wondering why the clerk had not asked him to sign in. He slugged his key into the lock and opened the door. "God, a real bed," Slade whispered.

The moon splintered through the open window of Slade's room in misty shadows. He was awakened by a rowdy bunch of mule skinners in the street below, shouting, swearing, looking for a fight, working off frustration after days of driving the mule trains full of supplies up and down the Santa Fe Trail.

Slade rolled over and went back to sleep, but was rattled awake again by a pounding on his door. He fell out of bed, clunked to the floor, and tried to orient himself. He hooked his arm up under the pillows and pulled down his Colt. He crawled to the window, peeked down into the alley. It was deserted. Then he called at the door. "Who is it?"

"Me, Sue O'Riley. Who else would it be?"

Slade got up and let her in, then slammed the door and locked it.

"God, you're jumpy," Sue said, flashing him a cute smile.

Slade stood in gray balbriggans, his Colt leveled at the pretty young girl. "What is it?"

"I came to talk with you. I told you we had somethin' to discuss."

She walked to his bed, sat on the edge, and crossed her legs. Her black skirt pulled up over black laced boots. She wore a pink satin blouse, and her hair was combed out under the flop of her big leather hat.

She looked good. Sexy. More like a woman now.

"What time is it?" Slade asked.

"Near midnight. You've been sleepin' a long time. I thought maybe it would be okay to come see you now."

Slade walked to the chiffonier. "Drink?" he asked.

Sue took her hat off, shook her hair out, and said, "No, thanks."

Slade poured two fingers into a barrel glass, swilled it around, knocked it down, then leaned against the chiffonier as the alcohol splashed through his lean frame, spread at first like molasses, then dumped with a rush into his empty belly.

Sue leaned over on the bed, took a box of Russell and Warrens from the table by the bed, and lit the oil lamp. Her breasts pushed into the soft satin of her tight blouse. She blew the match out and looked at Slade. Her cheeks were rouged, her lips red and invitingly juicy.

"You didn't have to get all dolled up to come and see me," Frank said.

"Oh, I didn't, Slade," Sue said quickly. "The professor and I are doin' our show in an hour or so."

"Your show?"

"Sure, the professor has already set up the wagon down on Main Street."

"Isn't it a little late for a medicine show?"

"We like to get 'em comin' out of the bars, a little drunk. You know, juiced up and feelin' like men. That's when we make the most money."

Slade poured another whiskey. "I see," he said.

"I wonder if you really do," Sue said, affecting a pouty look.

"You wanted to talk?"

"Yeah, about a couple things you might find interesting. Real interesting."

"Such as?"

Sue got up and walked slowly, sexily over to Slade, took the glass from him, licked her tongue over the rim, set it on the chiffonier, then wound her arms around Frank and pressed in, her body bending softly.

She was small, no more than five-three. Slade worked his hands in circles on the back of her satin blouse.

She looked up into his face. She smelled good, felt good. Her thin hips rolled into Frank, rotating on his lifting hardness.

Slade kissed her.

It was a warm, tender embrace. Sue pulled away, tucking her chin into her collarbone as she looked down at Frank's bulging balbriggans.

"Good grief, Slade," she whispered.

She reached down and unbuttoned the gray shorts and sliced her hand into the fly. The shorts floated down Slade's legs to his ankles.

Sue grabbed his hardness and squeezed the pulpy staff.

Slade unbuttoned her thin blouse. She wore a white corselet. He thumbed the straps down over her shoulders and cupped her plumlike breasts in his rough hands with gentleness and respect.

"Let's go do it on the bed," Sue said, her voice breathy and hot.

"Better than a cave floor," Slade suggested, following Sue to his bed. She stopped, stripped off her skirt, pulled the corselet over her head, and stood naked except for dark, gartered stockings and her laced boots.

She lay back on the bed.

Slade got up over her on his knees, straddling her little body. Sue lifted off the bed, her back arching like a cat. She clasped her hands behind Frank, clutching his tight butt, and held on for balance as her mouth opened.

Frank leveled his cock, and Sue craned forward, her red lips sealing around the hard stalk. She rocked back and forth, in and out, her back still curved off the bed, her hands pinching into Slade's butt.

He reached behind him, slid his hand down her belly and into the rich carpet of curls between her legs. She was wet and it was easy to part her. He pleasured her with his fingers and rocked back and forth with her.

Then he pushed Sue down on the bed. Her hair sprayed out on the pillow. Slade slid over her.

"Take it easy now, Slade. Remember, I'm tiny."

Frank fisted his hardness and pushed into her.

"Yeahhoooo." Sue sighed.

Once Slade had a good stroke going he said, "What did you have to tell me?"

Sue cocked her stockinged legs wide, lifted them, and circled Frank's rump. "I'll tell you, there's no hurry.

But you'll be surprised. Right now I want you to just keep screwin'.''

Slade slammed up and down. "What if I want to know right now?"

"You'd be a fool . . . push me some more."

Slade rolled his hips.

"Gawwwd!" Sue cried.

Frank worked her with long, slow slides. Sue pumped off the bed and undulated against him.

"That's enough, Slade," Sue whimpered.

She brought one hand to his head, ran her fingers through his thick black hair, grabbed a handful, and pulled.

"Okay, now! Go! Do it!" she wailed.

Slade held back. "Tell me," he whispered.

"Come on, don't!"

"Tell me!"

"Screw first."

"No, tell me."

"Please, Slade!"

Frank pumped harder, faster. He slid one hand under her rump and hooked his other arm under her neck. His face was inches from Sue's. Their eyes met. She pulled him down into a wild kiss.

Slade twisted away from her lips, slicked his tongue across her cheek, nibbled her ear. "Tell me now."

"God, this is good, Slade."

Frank wasn't about to let her play games with him. He stopped, held himself tense, rigid over her.

"Don't do that!" Sue yelped, rolling her hips furiously at his hardness.

"Tell me!"

"Okay, okay, just don't stop."

Slade picked up speed, thumping slowly at first, then faster and faster. His body whacked against Sue. She bounced off the bed to meet him. Then she stiffened. Her mouth came unhinged. She shuddered in wild, spasmodic jerks.

"Tell me!" Frank said, his voice rough through clenched teeth.

"I'm Pretty LaRue's daughter!" Sue yelled.

Chapter Twenty-one

Slade stood at the chiffonier and pulled on his jeans. Sue lay on the bed. He poured a generous splash of whiskey into his glass and did it in.

"That's a sweet little piece of news," he said, lighting a cheroot.

"I thought maybe it would interest you," Sue said, swinging to the side of the bed. She bent over and picked up her clothes and pulled on her corselet.

"Pretty's your mother?"

"Well, yes and no. She's my stepmother. Can I have one of those cheroots? I like to smoke after I do it."

Slade handed her his, then lit another.

"I'd like a drink too."

Slade poured her one in the other glass by the tin washbasin. Sue got up and took it from him. She went to the window and peered out.

"Full moon tonight," she said softly.

"You better tell me the story," Slade said, wondering if Pretty's stepdaughter had been in any way connected with Pretty bringing him back to Dodge City for hanging.

"It's a long one."

"I reckon I got time to hear it," Slade said.

Sue looked down into the street. "It was ten years ago. I was only nine. Pretty would have been in her early twenties. My pa had a farm near Iowa City. My mom died three years before of rheumatic fever. Pretty LaRue showed up one day and started working in a bar in Iowa City where all the farmers went on Saturday nights."

"My pa had a nice farm, good land. It was worth a lot. But he was vulnerable. Know what I mean?"

"Sure, he was lonely," said Slade, walking to the window. He took a position across from Sue on the other side. He sipped from his glass and looked down into the busy street below. It had turned warm, and the soft, autumn breeze felt good.

"And Pretty was a young, good-looking woman."

"I'd suppose she was," Slade said.

"Well, she was real nice to me. I liked her. We were happy again there on that farm. Life was good for a couple years."

"And?"

Sue looked up at Slade. "And . . . she killed my pa."

"*Killed* him?"

"Yes."

"How did that happen? Why wasn't she jailed?"

Sue chuckled. "You know her. She's clever."

Slade nodded. "I'd have to agree with that observation."

"Then you know how she is."

"Devious. Cunning."

"Yes, exactly. Well, she came into town, Dad fell for her and married her. And like I say, things were real good for a while. Then one day Pa was shoeing a horse in the barn. I saw Pretty go out there. I was playing over by the creek that ran by the house. She came out of the barn holding something. I didn't realize it at the time, but it was a hammer.

"A couple hours later I went into the barn and found my pa on the floor, his head all bashed in. He was stretched out there near the horse he'd just shoed. She must have snuck up on Pa and hit him with a hammer in the forehead as hard as she could. He was dead when I found him."

"Are you sure it was her?" Slade asked, crossing the small room to the chiffonier to fill their glasses with some more whiskey.

Sue turned and waited. Slade walked back to her, handed her the fresh whiskey, and resumed his place on the other side of the window from her.

"My dad knew how to shoe a horse, for Christ's sake. But I was so young. You know? Confused."

"I understand," Slade said, thinking about the day his mother and father had been killed by Langdon's men.

"Pa had signed Pretty into his will. The sheriff came out. They ruled it an accident. Killed by the horse, a kick in the head. Pretty got the farm. She sold it for a nice chunk of money, took me into Iowa City, and left me off on the street. I was just turning twelve."

"God, what did you do?" Slade asked, trying to be sensitive to her story, but wondering if it was really true.

"I can see you think I might be lyin'," Sue said.

"I'm careful," Slade replied.

"Can't blame you," she continued. "So Pretty took the money and just left me there. There wasn't much I could do. I turned to prostitution. I learned fast about men."

Slade nodded and sipped his whiskey.

"I stayed with two old whores and worked the streets until I was sixteen. Then I went back to school. I'd saved money. I got my high school diploma and enrolled in the university.

"But I never forgot about Pretty LaRue. Always, in the back of my mind, I thought I'd find her and pay her back for what she did to me and my pa. Like what you did to Langdon."

They stood for a moment in silence. Voices and yelling from the street below filtered up into the room. The creak of buggies, the pounding of hoofbeats echoed in the night.

"I gotta hurry and get back to the professor," Sue said.

"How'd you get tied up with him?" Slade asked.

"I was at the university. He came through Iowa City with his show."

Sue paused, took a drink, puffed on her cheroot, and looked over at Slade. "College wasn't much for me. Just a bunch of women who wanted to be teachers. I'd had years on the streets. I was smarter than they were.

"Anyway, I was on my way to class. I stopped to

watch the professor. He had a compelling pitch, know what I mean?''

"Don't underestimate me," Slade said.

"He came up to me, slipped me five double eagles, and said, 'How would you like to earn this much every week?' This was just about the time I'd read in the paper that Pretty had been involved in your capture, that they were takin' you back to Dodge City. It's the first I'd heard 'bout her since she killed my dad.''

"So you took up with the professor?"

"Why not? I saw a chance to get out of Iowa, a chance to find Pretty LaRue. I thought maybe she'd be in Dodge.''

Slade lifted the window higher to air out the smoke. "What if she had been?"

"I would have found a way to kill her."

"I suppose you would have," Slade conjectured.

"Pretty was too smart to stick around. She took that reward money and lit out."

Slade nodded.

"Where did you meet her, Slade?"

"In Horseshoe Flats, up north of the Black Hills. She was singing in a bar there.''

"Hiding out from somethin' probably."

"Well, now that you've told your story, I wouldn't deny that.''

"She's a witch."

"But she saved my life. She nursed me back to health after I'd been wounded in a gunfight.''

"Yeah, then she turned on you in Yankton. The paper said she and Bat Masterson caught you. I'll bet I know how.''

"She tricked me," Slade said.

Sue chuckled sarcastically. "She's good at that. Anyway, I put in with the professor. We headed west, working the small towns, the settlements, making good money. I'm the shill. I draw the crowd. He sells the shit. And I've been doin' good, Slade."

"That doesn't surprise me."

But when we finally got to Dodge City, Pretty had left. Now, I'm out here on the trail with the professor, making money, but I have no idea where Pretty LaRue is. Do you?"

Slade shook his head.

"But you're gonna be lookin' for her, right? After what she did to you?"

"I'll be keepin' my eyes open, that's for sure," Slade said.

"I figured you would, and I'm willing to make you a deal to keep a keen watch for her."

"What kind of deal?"

"You find her, you kill her, and I'll pay you a thousand dollars," Sue said, looking up, staring into Slade's face with determination.

"I've never killed a woman."

"Yeah? Well, I wouldn't let that bother you. She tried to hang you, and she pounded my dad to death. She's like a poison snake."

Slade could hear the hate in Sue's voice.

She continued. "I've had a lot of experience with men in my young life, Slade." Sue emphasized "young" as if to send more hate toward Pretty LaRue for cheating her out of her father's farm, for leaving her orphaned on an Iowa City street.

"See, Slade, there's a kind of man who tends to

forget and forgive too easily. I don't want you to do that."

"I don't think I can in this case. She turned me in to hang."

"If I find her first I'll kill her. I'm goin' with the professor on down the Trail to Las Vegas, Santa Fe, then we're gonna work west. If I find her, if I run into her, I'll kill her, Slade."

"I'm sure you will."

Sue gave Frank a smile. "Bet that tight, good-lookin' butt of yours on it, Slade."

Frank laughed.

"You know," Sue continued, her voice soft, more serious, "I tried to come see you in Dodge City before the hanging, but they wouldn't let me in. I wanted to talk to you about Pretty. We left the same morning you broke out with the lawyer. The town was so all fired up and concerned about you, they forgot they had the professor under suspicion. I knew who you were the minute you crawled into that cave up on Simpson's Rest."

"Why didn't you tell me about all this sooner?" Slade asked.

"God, are you kiddin', and have the professor bugging me about it the rest of the trip? Listen, I'm just using him as a means to get out to California."

"This thousand dollars you're payin'," Slade said, "you payin' that now?"

"Five hundred now, five hundred when I know you've killed her."

"I wouldn't take money for somethin' like this under normal circumstances, seeing that I want Pretty as badly as you do, Sue, but I'm short. I need cash. I need a stake to move on. I got the law after me. I'll take it as a loan."

"You get five hundred right now," Sue said. She flicked her cheroot out the window. Slade watched the red tip spiral to the street, bounce, shoot sparks, and die in the gutter.

"There's a man in Rapid City, up in Dakota Territory. His name is Peterson. You can contact me through him. I'll be in touch with him from time to time. He's a gunsmith there. If I find Pretty, I'll let him know."

"Good. I was wonderin' how we'd be keepin' touch, Slade."

Sue reached into a slit in her skirt and pulled out a roll of greenbacks. "Here's the five hundred."

"You sure now about this?" Slade asked.

Sue sat down on the edge of the bed and looked up incredulously at Slade. "I want Pretty LaRue to pay for what she done to my pa and me. I want her to pay just like you do."

"Okay, it's a deal," Frank said, taking the money.

"There's one thing, Slade."

"Yes?"

"If you find her I want you to make it slow, make her think about what she did."

"I'll keep that in mind," Slade said, walking with her to the door.

Sue turned. "The professor and I never stay long in one place, lest they catch on to the ruse, so I guess this is good-bye, unless you come down and catch our show. I dance a little, draw the men. The professor tells 'em I'll strip if they buy. We sell the shit, then we move out."

She hugged Frank. "Nice meetin' you, Slade. Don't forget you've got five hundred dollars of mine."

"You have my word. If I find Pretty, I'll take care of her like you asked."

She looked at him. "Sure, if she doesn't take care of you first, like she did back there in Yankton."

Sue turned and walked down the hall.

Chapter Twenty-two

Lady Fortune's wheel was spinning again. One episode after another. Slade wondered if he might not be living in a dream. A nasty nightmare. The bank robbery in Rochford, the encounter with Red Dog, Pretty LaRue in Yankton, the hanging rope in Dodge City, the strange experiences up on Simpson's Rest, and Sue O'Riley's request to kill Pretty LaRue.

Trouble.

But trouble made a man strong, and Slade knew one thing. He had to stay tough, even if he felt he was going up against the whole world. He couldn't give up and wouldn't.

He dressed and went down Commercial Street and walked past a Harvey House.

The hot plateau sun had turned the night warm. Slade walked Main Street to the Rimrock Saloon. He slid through the bat-wing doors and shouldered his way through the crowd and smoke to the bar.

He found a place and slipped into it, got the bartender's attention. "Sweet Home?"

"Nope."

"Jim Beam?"

"Nope. Got some Even Williams."

Slade nodded. "Bring me a shot glass and the bottle."

The apron pushed the bottle to Slade with a shot glass. "Only bottle of Even we got," he said.

Frank poured one and put it down. He had another quick shot, then leaned in, elbows on the bar, and waited for the liquor to juice him.

He found himself scanning the crowd for Pretty LaRue, while he listened to two men drinking hard and talking next to him.

"They been blastin' into pure silver up there," one of the men said.

The other sipped a watery glass of beer and wiped the foam from his mustache. "I heard their sluices have been clogged with thick carbonate of lead carrying forty ounces of silver to the ton."

"It's the biggest silver strike ever," said another man, pushing up to the bar.

"We better get up there. Levi Leiter, the man that owns Marshall Field Company in Chicago, just bought out Alvinus Wood for forty thousand dollars and turned a dozen claims into two million within a week."

Slade listened closely.

"Meyer Guggenheim's over there too."

"See? You know when the big boys start to buy things

up you got a rich find, and they got a doozy up there in Leadville.''

"Plain old prospectors like us been hittin' pure veins. I'm talkin' about pure silver.''

Slade poured another straight shot and sipped slowly.

"It ain't that far from here,'' a crusty-looking man said. "I'm goin' up before winter sets in. No one will get there after the bad snows. It'll be a monopoly for the miners already there.''

"They say it's a better strike than they had last year in Deadwood.''

Slade had heard enough. There was nothing like a new strike, a bustling new mining town for a man on the run. The flood of strangers was easy to get lost in, and the law was usually loose, if there was any at all.

Frank walked the long bar, worked down the counter. All the talk was about the silver find in Leadville to the north, up around the headwaters of the Arkansas River.

Slade was suddenly shocked back into reality. He'd seen enough of the man's back, the way his long hair curled on his collar, the tan Stetson, to know that it was Bat Masterson who stood at the bar just ahead.

Frank thanked his spin of luck, to get Bat looking the other way, and he was quick to act. He slipped up behind the lawman and pulled his Colt. He shoved the barrel into Bat's back. "Lookin' for me, Bat?''

Masterson tensed, recognizing the voice. He didn't move or attempt to look over his shoulder.

"You know what they say about me, Bat. I'm a ruthless, sadistic killer. Take that into account and listen good to me now.''

Slade waited a moment, pushed his gun harder into Bat's back.

"You'll walk away from the bar. You'll keep your hands in your coat pockets. One move and I'll end all those stories about you. Nod if you understand me."

Bat slowly tipped his head up and down. He left the bar, his hands tucked in his black coat. Slade followed, his gun holstered now.

Bat bulled through the swinging doors, Slade right behind him. Frank pulled the Colt again.

"Walk down Main Street, keep close to the buildings, in the shadows. Lead me to your horse. Is it in the livery?"

"No," Bat said. "I hitched it over on Maple Street on the edge of town. I wanted to look around first."

"You were lookin' the wrong way in that bar, son."

They walked to Maple Street. It was dark, deserted, and had only three residences dotting the sideway. They found Masterson's horse. Bat still had his back to Slade.

"Now slowly, very slowly, take your gun out of your holster with your thumb and forefinger, and drop it to the ground."

Masterson did as instructed, and Slade took Bat's lariat from the horse. He tied the lawman to a tree down the street near the Purgatoire, gagged him, and stepped back.

"I could shoot you now, couldn't I?" Slade said.

Bat nodded.

"I guess you'll wait there for a while. I'll be back in a few minutes. We're gonna take a ride."

Slade hurried to the livery. He didn't have time to waste or to dicker with the old man who attended him.

"I need a good, strong Appaloosa," Slade said.

"Ain't got one."

"Yes, you have," said Slade, pointing to the horse.

"Not for sale. Belongs to my son."

"I'll pay well. I need a good mountain horse."

"Goin' up to Leadville?"

"Yes."

"Could be my son would sell, but he ain't around right now. You could dicker with him tomorrow."

"Then I'll rent tonight. How 'bout that gelding?"

"No. Just castrated. He ain't ready to run right yet."

"I'll take the chestnut, then."

"Have it back tonight?"

"Early morning."

"Four bits."

Frank paid the old man. "Listen, I'll need saddle, bridle, the whole rig tomorrow when I come to buy the Appaloosa."

"I can accommodate you."

The old man helped Slade saddle up and he rode out of the livery, back down Maple Street to the river where he had the famous Bat Masterson tied to a tree.

Frank rode up and dismounted. He untied Masterson and said, "Now, strip off all your clothes, Bat."

"Huh?"

"Do as I say. Right now. Take your clothes off."

"Aw, shit, Slade, there ain't no—"

"As you told me so often, Bat, 'Can it!' " Slade shouted.

Bat shrugged and stripped naked.

"Now, up on your horse."

"Shit, Slade, come on. What is goin' on?"

"Up, and right now. Then ride east along the Purgatoire."

Masterson rode ahead of Slade. The moon was high

and bright. Frank stayed close behind as they rode the river back toward the Kansas line.

They had pushed hard for two hours when Bat slowed down. "Slade, we gotta stop. The horse is giving out."

Frank pulled up beside Masterson. "Okay, out of the saddle."

Bat slipped down. Slade dismounted. He cracked the ass of Bat's horse, sent him trotting off into the night, fired two shots to send the horse into a gallop, then turned to the naked lawman.

"Here's the way I see it, Masterson. It'll take you a couple hours to catch up with your horse and find him. By then it will be morning. If you ride back into Trinidad, you'll be comin' in naked under the sun. Might be embarrassing seeing the reputation you been building. 'Course, by the time you got back into town, I'd be gone anyway.

"Or I can shoot you and leave you dead. No one would know.

"Or you can catch up with your horse and find yourself some clothes, then ride back into Dodge City and tell them you couldn't find me.

"You do that, Bat, and I'll forget this embarrassing night ever happened.

"Now I'm ruling out killing you, because you see, Masterson, I'm not the ruthless killer they make me out to be in Dodge. I'm innocent of those charges, and I think you suspect I might be.

"And I'm figuring you don't want me to kill you, right, Bat?"

"Go ahead if you want to."

Frank pulled his Colt. He clicked the hammer. "Sure, why not? I don't owe you a damn thing."

"Now wait a minute, Slade. There's no sense in—"

"See, I didn't think you wanted to die, Bat. Not naked out here on the Jornado. Bad ending to your legend. So, I'll leave you and wish you good luck."

"Whatever I do, I ain't gonna forget this, Slade," Bat said.

"Just start walking. You lose this round."

Bat took off in a fast stride.

"Hey, Bat!"

"Yeah?"

"You look cute naked," Slade hollered, then mounted his chestnut and galloped back toward Trinidad. He'd lost a lot of time, but it had been worth it just to see Bat Masterson eat shit.

Chapter Twenty-three

Frank arrived back in Trinidad in the middle of the night. He was thankful it was an all-night town. He needed a few drinks.

He went to his room and washed the dust off, then walked back into the night. He stopped abruptly, his body tensed. He adjusted the Colt Peacemaker, cuddled the handle in his palm and fingers. No matter what tricks life played, no matter how many episodes he had to endure, including the random swings of Fortune's wheel, Slade always had his Peacemaker. A ripple of security spilled through him. Back in his room he had the Goodnight Winchester and his nitrate caps. He took a deep breath, relaxed his coiled body, and continued down the street.

Slade needed a card game. He wanted to see if he could work Sue's five hundred dollars into a good stake for Leadville.

He walked in the glow of the naphtha lamps until he came to the Stockman's Saloon and Card Hall. He went in and ordered a whiskey.

"Got Jim Beam?"

"Cost you extra."

"I want the bottle," Slade said.

He poured and glanced about the saloon. The poker tables were off to the left side.

Frank took the bottle and shot glass and walked over. He watched awhile and decided the table in the back would suit his purpose. Two stockmen and a young cowboy in a fancy gray suit, red vest, black Stetson, and handmade boots were having a friendly game.

Slade pulled out an empty chair. "May I join, gentlemen?"

They gave him the once-over and nodded.

The oldest player, a grizzly rancher, said, "It's five-dollar ante, seven-card stud, no wild cards. Twenty-dollar limit. Three bumps."

Frank slid a gold half eagle onto the table. A rancher across from him in a buckskin vest and gray beard dealt around.

Up cards around were all low, four of hearts, six of hearts, deuce of hearts, and Frank had an eight of spades. He had a king of spades and a nine of diamonds in the hole.

"Stranger is high with the eight of spades," the dealer said.

Frank laid one of Sue's wrinkled bills on the table. "Bets five bucks."

They called around. Slade counted the pot. Forty dollars.

The dealer spit the cards around the table again, skipping them over the burnished surface. There was no help for anyone, including Frank, who hooked the queen of clubs.

"You're still high, stranger."

"Five more," said Slade. The players called and the pot increased to sixty dollars.

The dealer spun the cards. Nothing much happening. The fancy cowboy had a possible straight working with a deuce, eight, and four up. Slade drew a five of hearts. No help. The two ranchers had low cards going nowhere.

But there were always two hole cards down, so it was difficult in any game of seven-card stud to really tell what was happening.

"You're still high," the dealer said, nodding at Slade.

Frank was bluffing, of course, taking a long shot he could hook something up with the two cards he had coming. "Another five," he said.

"I'm calling one more damn time, that's all," said the old rancher.

The dealer sent the cards flying. "Absolutely no help for you, Jesse," he said, sliding him a queen of diamonds. "And, kid, you're workin' on a nice little straight there. You need a good hit . . . ah, how's that? A tray of diamonds. Got the deuce, eight, four, three showing. Is he hooked up in the hole?"

Then he dealt Slade the king of clubs. "No help there, sir," he said, laying his own cards down in front of him. "A seven of clubs. Shit!"

"You're still high, sir," he said to Slade.

"Five bucks," Slade said, more confident now with his pair of kings.

Everyone called. The pot was one hundred dollars.

"Okay, down and dirty," the dealer said, whipping the last card to each hand down.

Everyone checked his hole cards.

"You are still high," the dealer said to Slade.

"Five more."

"I'm foldin'," Jesse said.

"I'll call, what the hell," said the dealer.

The fancily dressed kid smiled and said, "I'll raise five."

"And five more," Slade mumbled.

The kid and Slade kept bumping each other, and the dealer kept calling, until the pot was well over two hundred dollars.

Since they'd called Slade on his last bet, he turned over his hole cards first. "Pair of kings," he said, lighting a cheroot.

"I didn't have shit," said the dealer. "Just a pair of sevens."

"I couldn't hit that damn straight, and a pair of fours showin' doesn't do me any good against those kings," the kid said.

Frank pulled in the pot. He sat back and smoked his cigar. He was good at bluffing, building a bad hand into a winner. Most gamblers drop out if their first three or four cards aren't playing to a winning hand. Frank liked to stay with it, work the draw.

He lost a game, then won again, and finally pulled in a jacks-or-better jackpot worth over three hundred dollars.

The oldest rancher stood up and yawned. "Well, that does it for me. Gettin' late."

"Me too," the dealer said. "Be daylight soon."

Slade was glad the game was breaking up. With the

money Sue had paid him, plus his poker winnings, Slade had over a thousand dollars, enough to buy the Appaloosa and a rig, enough to make a start in Leadville.

The young cowboy leaned forward. "Never did get your name," he said to Slade.

"Didn't give it."

"I'm Bunker. Bunker Morningside."

"Big deal," said Slade.

The remark jolted the youngster. He didn't look more than twenty-one. He stiffened, then leaned closer across the table, his eyebrows arching.

"I'll cut you for your winnings," Morningside said.

Frank checked him out further. Handsome, square chin, strong eyes, his Stetson on a cocky tilt.

Slade counted out gold and paper, pushed it to the middle of the table. "Let's cut for a thousand."

"Good, that's good, more than your winnings, huh?"

"Just match my pot."

"Is my check good?"

Frank reached for his money, started to drag in the big pot he'd placed on the table.

"Now wait a minute. What are you doin' there?"

"No checks," Slade said coldly.

The kid called the bartender. "Ed, come here."

The apron ambled lazily from behind the bar to the one remaining poker table. "Yeah, Bunker?"

"Ed, get Dean Sorenson," the lad said, then looked over at Slade. "Sorenson is the banker here in Trinidad."

"It's awful late, or early, to be gettin' Mr. Sorenson up, Bunker."

"Goddammit, Ed, do as I say!" the kid shouted, turning with an angry face to the bartender.

Frank had two shots of whiskey while he waited in silence with his opponent. A woman came up to the table. She had long blond hair with ringlets. She was packed into a tight red dress. Slade could tell she was tightly corseted underneath. Her waist was tiny. The boned bodice of her dress lifted her breasts so they fluffed out on the low-cut sweep.

Her face was hard. But there was a mysterious sparkle in her eyes.

She stood behind the kid.

The bat-wing doors to the saloon swung open. A dignified man, who had obviously been asleep and not had a chance to dress properly, walked in. He wore a blue serge suit, sloppy white shirt, no tie, shoes with no socks.

"Your daddy's not gonna like this, Bunker," the banker said as he slid into a chair at the table. He offered Bunker a draft and a handful of greenbacks.

The kid signed it, took the money, and matched Slade's bet. The people remaining in the saloon had already gathered around the table. Frank felt good. He loved gambling. Why not? Wasn't his life a gamble, just a spin of Fortune's wheel?

Frank and the kid looked at each other across the table. Slade needed the money. He figured the kid didn't.

Bunker Morningside smiled. "Let's have a fresh deck, Ed," he said.

The bartender brought a pack of new cards, laid them on the table. All the time Slade was looking at the woman in red. She smiled and stared back at him.

"Want 'em shuffled?" Bunker asked. "Or you wanna cut off the new deck?"

"I think we should let someone impartial shuffle, like the pretty lady there in red," Slade said.

"Oh, Janelle. Sure. Janelle can cut," Morningside said, smiling. "I trust her."

Janelle nodded at the men. She sat down. Her big boobs bobbled in the lift of the décolleté dress. Her red fingertips worked quickly and professionally as she shuffled the cards. Then she fanned them out on the table.

Bunker Morningside pulled one and turned over the king of diamonds. He let out a long sigh of relief, a winner's sigh, and slumped back into his chair.

"I'll let the lady cut for me," Slade said, then looked up at her. "Lady luck," he added.

Janelle's bright red fingertips tapped out to the fanned cards, she pulled one, then snapped it over on the green felt.

"Ace of diamonds," she said.

"Aw, shit!" the kid howled.

The banker heaved back into his chair. The crowd buzzed.

Frank pulled in the pot.

The game broke up. Slade had won his stake, but he knew he'd have to pay Janelle. After all, she had stacked the cut in Slade's favor. She knew all the time where the aces were.

Morningside left the saloon, his head hanging. Janelle went to the bar. Slade bagged the money and got up. He walked over to the woman and slid in beside her.

"How much did that cut cost me?" he whispered.

Janelle turned and smiled up at Slade. "I'll take two hundred for my trouble," she said.

"Ouch!" Frank mumbled.

"Hey, come on, you got a good win out of it."

"You're right," Slade said. "But you cheated, Janelle."

"Of course I did. Serves the little bastard right. And
his pa. They been cheating cattlemen on prices long
enough around here. Makes me feel good to screw 'em
a little. They got the money."

"Where'd you learn that shuffle?" Slade asked.

Janelle poured herself a drink, turned, and faced
Slade. "For me to know and you to find out, my friend.
What's your name?"

"Bill," said Slade.

"Sure it is, just like my name's Janelle."

Slade took his roll out, peeled off two hundred dollars
discreetly under the bar, and handed it to Janelle. She
palmed the money and tucked it down into the top of
her dress.

"It's all business, isn't it?" Janelle said.

"When it comes down to money," Slade answered.

Janelle smiled. "That's the way I see it, Slade, and if
you might be lookin' for Pretty LaRue she left a week
ago."

The simple mention of Pretty's name riled Slade.
This, coupled with the fact that Janelle knew who he
was, sent a coiled shiver through Slade.

"I might or might not be who you call me, but I don't
know anyone named Pretty LaRue."

Janelle's smile widened. "Sure you do, and so do I.
We both know Pretty LaRue, and we both know you're
Frank Slade."

"If you knew all that, why didn't you turn me in, call
the law on me instead of taking two hundred dollars?"

"Well, we all got a past, haven't we, Slade? You're
Bill, I'm Janelle. You think that's my real name?"

Slade relaxed. "You mentioned Pretty LaRue? How do you know her?"

"Worked with her in Kansas City. She was flush with money. She'd just left Iowa, said she was on her way to Denver for a singing career. She showed up here in town a week ago, and we talked over old times."

"How'd you know who I was?" Slade asked.

"Oh, shit, Slade, I was in Deadwood last year when you were. Everyone there knew who you were."

"Did Pretty say where she might be going?" Slade said, moving in closer to Janelle.

"Now, Slade," Janelle whispered, "you wouldn't expect me, a businesswoman and such, to give out that kind of information without a token of appreciation. Would you?"

Slade hated to let go of any more winnings, but he was quick to respond. "How much, Janelle?"

"Another hundred."

Slade reached back into his pocket. He pulled out his greenback roll. He had the gold in his other pocket. He flipped off the hundred dollars.

Janelle took the money under the bar, and again she pushed it down into the top of her dress.

"She said something about Leadville, doing some singing there, then moving on up to Denver again to the Brown Palace."

"Much obliged," Slade said, then pushed away from the bar. He looked down into Janelle's face. "I could kill you, Janelle, right now, get my money back, and not have to worry about you tellin' the law about me."

"Oh, but you won't do that, Slade," Janelle said, turning to face him, sliding her elbows back on the bar, heaving out her huge tits.

—175—

"Yeah? And why won't I, Janelle?"

" 'Cause Pretty said you were a terrific guy. She really raved about you."

"Sure she did," Slade said sarcastically.

"No, she did, Slade. She said you were a good man."

Slade shook his head and smiled. "The bullshit around here is gettin' so deep I might drown in it."

Ed, the bartender, walked up. "Look, goddammit, let's close up for an hour or two so I can clean the place."

"Sure, Ed," Janelle said.

She turned to Slade, touched his arm, and said, "See you around, Bill."

Slade watched the wiggle of her plush hips as she walked away. He called out to her, "Sure, see you around, Janelle."

Slade felt good. He had a stake. He packed his possibles in the break of the early morning, filled his saddlebags, and hauled his gear to the livery stable. He purchased the strong Appaloosa, a good mountain climber, bought a saddle and bridle, cinched the horse, and rode down Main Street to Billson's General Store.

He stopped in and bought a poncho, two blankets, gloves, plenty of canned beans, jerky, parched corn, an ax, a lariat, and rigged himself out all the way for his trip north.

By the time he was ready to leave Trinidad the sky had darkened. Big black thunderheads were bellying in off the mountains. The wind turned cold. Frank stopped at the end of Main Street and slipped into the poncho, then heeled his horse toward the Rockies.

Slade had no illusions. He knew by now Cliff Langdon or the authorities would have someone out after him.

Maybe Bat Masterson would be back on his trail. But he had a head start, and Leadville sounded like the kind of place he could hit it big, make it quick, then move on.

Would Pretty LaRue be there as Janelle had said, or had the bar girl lied? And why would Pretty be talking about him like he was a hero? Frank figured she'd have to do some fancy talking if she were to stop him from killing her.

A light rain fell. Slade pushed the Appaloosa faster. His poncho lifted behind him. The temperature dropped. He hoped he could make Leadville before the blizzards set in again.

Epilogue

Niles Caldwell hunkered over the bar in the Drover's Hotel in Abilene. He licked the foam off the top of his beer mug, then gulped the rich, brown brew. He had his arm around a girl who pressed into his thigh.

Caldwell was twenty-seven, lean but muscular. He was short, maybe five-six. He had sinister blue eyes and thick sandy hair. He was dressed in a tan suit with a blue vest.

A fat man with a green visor on his forehead rushed through the saloon crowd and made his way to Caldwell.

"Niles Caldwell?" he called.

Niles turned.

"Niles Caldwell!"

"Over here," Niles said.

"Telegram from Dodge City."

Niles took the wire and opened it.

Come to Dodge City right away. Need your help in taking Frank Slade. Reward and bonus. Hurry!
Cliff Langdon, Mayor

"What is it, Niles?" the girl asked, looking into Caldwell's baby face.

His cheeks were flushed, his skin smooth.

Niles read the telegram and said, "Cliff Langdon down in Dodge. He wants to see me."

"Cliff Langdon sent *you* a telegram, Niles?"

Caldwell laid the wire on the bar. The girl read it, then looked up at him. "God, Niles, you get in with Langdon and you got a future in Kansas."

"Don't I know it," Niles said.

"And Frank Slade, you can take him, huh, Niles?"

Caldwell was cocky. He was quick. He smiled at the girl. "Oh, I think there's a way. I think there's a real easy way to take Slade."

He turned and walked away.

"Hey, Niles, you have to leave right now?" the girl called.

Caldwell didn't hear her. He had one thing on his mind. Get to Dodge City. Find out what kind of deal Cliff Langdon had to offer, then go after Frank Slade, after a pile of money and a chance for fame.

Niles Caldwell was ready for both.

Watch for

Layover In Leadville

*next in the exciting Slade series
coming soon from Lynx Books!*